Frederik Sandwich and the Mayor Who Lost Her Marbles

Also by Kevin John Scott

Frederik Sandwich and the Earthquake that Couldn't Possibly Be

Frederik Sandwich and the Mayor Who Lost Her Marbles

Kevin John Scott

sourcebooks
young readers

Published by Sourcebooks Young Readers, an imprint of Sourcebooks Kids.
P.O. Box 4410, Naperville, Illinois 60567-4410
(630) 961-3900
sourcebookskids.com

Library of Congress Cataloging-in-Publication data is on file with the publisher.

Source of Production: Berryville Graphics, Inc., Berryville, Virginia, United States
Date of Production: March 2019
Run Number: 5014473

Printed and bound in the United States of America.
BVG 10 9 8 7 6 5 4 3 2 1

For Milo, Jessie, Niamh, and Erin.

May you light up the world like fireworks!

Two Short Weeks Before Her Ladyship the Mayor's International Midsummer Festival

On Frederik's Hill by King Frederik's Park in an orderly office high in Municipal Hall, there stood a woman: A serious woman who people took seriously. A woman of position, a woman of influence. A woman in a very bad mood.

"What the flipping festering devil," she demanded, "is *this*?"

She flung the morning newspaper across her desk.

Her desk was enormous. Enormous and orderly. The paper slid all the way across and fell off the other side onto her enormous, orderly floor.

Two tall detectives in identical, dark suits stared down at it. One of them cleared his throat a bit, but neither dared say a word.

Her Ladyship the Mayor of Frederik's Hill turned to her window in a fury. Her window was broad and high and spotlessly clean. Frederik's Square lay below her, a fountain at its heart. The finest stores and delicatessens lined Frederik's Avenue. Factory chimneys and the massive cylindrical vats of the brewery stood proud on her skyline. All of Her Ladyship's sources of revenue, taxes, and tariffs stretched before her. Frederik's Hill was an economic marvel, respected near and far. Thanks to her. It had taken years. Decades, in fact. Patience and grit. A ruthless attention to detail. And no one—*no one*—was going to get in her way. Not now, when she was so tantalizingly close to her long-awaited payoff.

One of the detectives retrieved the paper. "'Children Flee from Zombies,'" he read.

She placed her fingertips on the enormous, orderly desk. "Zombies!" she shouted.

"I didn't know we had any," the detective said.

"We don't!"

"No. Right. Of course. But it's on the front page, Your Ladyship."

"I am well aware which page it's on," she barked. "If I say there are no zombies, there are no zombies. I want to know who allowed this to be printed."

The detectives shuffled their feet and inspected their toes.

"Thomas is the editor, ma'am, as you know. Thomas Dahl Dalby. But he's loyal. Totally trustworthy. If Thomas says there are zombies, there must be something behind it. I wonder where he got the story from?"

Her Ladyship scowled and snarled. "From a fantasist. A saboteur. I want the presses stopped. I want the internet erased. Is that clear? I want all references to zombies rooted out and removed!"

"Like before, ma'am? With the earthquake?"

"Yes, exactly like that. This is catastrophic."

Her Ladyship caught herself grinding her teeth again. Her dentist had told her not to. But despite her position and all her staff, it seemed she *still* had to take care of everything herself.

Two months had passed since an accidental "earthquake" almost derailed her glide toward international fame. Every day since, she had fought to restore the right impression. Impressions were everything. She'd appeared on TV, online, and on the radio, radiating calm. She had spoken at meetings and malls, paving the way for her Midsummer Festival, creating a buzz. Souvenir programs were in the stores. Little, decorative flags fluttered above the streets. All mention, all *notion,* of anything untoward had been thoroughly buried. Her mishap with the fountains, her humiliation in front of the zoological society—silenced. Until this!

She drummed her fingers on the polished desktop.

"That moronic elephant keeper," she growled. "He was mumbling about zombies. Remember? During that nightmarish meeting at the zoo."

"We don't talk about that, Your Ladyship."

"I know we don't! But now we do. Is that clear?"

"Erm, right. Yes. No."

"Did it leak?"

"No, Your Ladyship. No, no. Not a peep."

"Are you sure?" Far too many respectable voters had witnessed her embarrassment—nasty kids confronting her, an elephant peeing all over her shoes and her spotless public image.

"Absolutely. Definitely. We spoke to everybody who was there, face-to-face, one-on-one, eye-to-eye. Told them *exactly* what would happen if they talked. We put a lid on the whole thing. Sealed it up, ma'am. Sank it like an elephant in a lake."

She glared at the detective. Mortensen. Or was it Martensen? It didn't matter. "You got to *everyone* who was there? Without exception? What about that Hotdog hoodlum?"

"We caught up with him next day, Your Ladyship," the other detective said. "He parks his cart by the ice rink. He wasn't hard to find."

Her Ladyship stiffened. "He parks a hot dog cart by the ice rink? At the entrance to the Garden Park? The main entrance?"

"That's right, ma'am."

"That's entirely *wrong*!" Heat was rushing to her face now. Her jaw ached from the grinding. "My festival guests are going to use that entrance. The ambassadors, the foreign VIPs, the queen! I will not have a filthy peddler waving hot dogs at the queen!"

"Of course. We'll deal with that."

"Do it now!"

"We'll close him down, ma'am. Revoke his license. He'll never sell a sausage in a public place again. We should have thought of that before."

"You should have thought of that before!"

"We should have."

"You should have!"

She snatched the paper from the detective's hand and stared at the headline again.

"Zombies!" she yelled. "Again! And children!" And a thought struck her. A horrible thought. "There were children at the zoo. The ones who appeared from nowhere. The tall one and the short one. What about them? What happened to them?"

"Ah," said Martensen—or was it Mortensen? "Never actually identified, Your Ladyship. Actually. Tricky, that one, actually. Erm. Not seen since, you see. Long gone. Over the hills and far away. But they won't be back. They weren't even local. You could tell just by looking at them."

Her Ladyship glared at each detective in turn. "Then how did this *zombie* hysteria get out? Tell me that!"

"We'll find out, Your Ladyship. We'll track it to the source and deal with it."

"*Thoroughly*, this time."

"Understood."

"Ruthlessly!"

"Got it."

"You are authorized to use whatever means are necessary. *Whatever* means."

The detectives nodded, exchanged a glance, and were reluctant to meet her eye.

"Is there a problem?" she demanded. "Are you too squeamish for this? Mortensen? Martensen?"

"No problem, Your Ladyship. No problem at all."

"Then get on with it."

She turned her back on them, dismissing them with a wave of her hand. She watched from her window as buses and bicycles puttered by, far below, on her busy, prosperous streets. The morning haze was burning away. Flags curled in the cool summer breeze. Beyond the buildings, the long, green sweep of the Garden Park stretched all the way up to the castle on the hill.

Two more weeks.

Just two more weeks of preparations, planning, and publicity. Two short weeks until her International Midsummer Festival—the fireworks, the VIPs, fine local cuisine. No fountains, to her great frustration. She'd been forced to abandon that plan. But Her Majesty the Queen would be there, and the eyes of the world would fall upon Frederik's Hill—and on Her Ladyship, at last.

"Zombies," she muttered in cold fury. "Zombies!"

Nothing would get in her way. Nothing and no one.

Reckless Miss Adventure

"Muffin!"

Again?

"Yoo-hoo, muffin, dear!"

Seriously? It wasn't that Frederik Sandwich disliked Pernille's company. Wasn't that at all. But there was such a surprising amount of her company to cope with. He was heading home now. He'd said goodbye. He was hurrying down the pedestrian walkway from Frederik's Shopping Mall toward Frederik's Hospital. It wasn't the quickest route home, but it was out of sight of Municipal Hall. These days, they steered clear of Municipal Hall. Anyone might be watching from those windows.

"Let's climb the new observation tower," called Pernille.

"It's three hundred years old. It isn't new."

"But it's newly opened to the public."

"No. I need to go and do something."

"What thing?"

"Anything. A thing. Some things. Does it matter what things?"

"Everything you do matters to me, muffin. I've got your back. I am the marvelous Miss Adventure, and you are my sidekick. You may be a mini-sized, funny-talking misfit, but you are the Toto to my Dorothy, the sandwich to my soup."

"Good grief."

"Go on. It'll only take a few minutes."

The tower was dead ahead, a stout cylinder of brickwork, ancient lettering on its face. Narrow, arched windows were sparsely spaced around its sides. The mayor had opened it one week ago—part of her campaign to impress the world. A prelude to her International Midsummer Festival on Frederik's Hill.

"No. We can't," he said. "It's too risky."

The mayor was as popular as ever, the earthquake all

but forgotten. Hardly anyone understood how dangerous she was. She might have cameras up in that tower. Listening devices. Spies and informers.

"But it's so deliciously tempting," Pernille said. "Think of the views from up there, above the rooftops, looking out across the Garden Park."

And she was right. They'd be able to see the city beyond with all its spires and domes. Maybe catch a glimpse of the suspension bridge in the far distance stretching over the sea to another country.

"Just a peek, muffin. You know you want to."

"No. We can't. And my name is not 'muffin'. How many times have I told you?"

"But I like muffins. Much more than sandwiches. And I like you too. Ergo, de facto. Sorry, but there it is."

He hurried on, head down, hoping she would give up. He was done for today. Enough of her endless chatter. Apartment blocks rose six floors ahead of him. Early summer sunlight bounced off their windows. Raucous children ran around with ice creams. Bicycles whizzed by, freewheeling riders laughing out loud. Frederik kept walking. Didn't look back. Refused to.

Where was she now?

He wouldn't look. It would only encourage her. Was she behind him? She was bound to be. Right on his heels.

Bother it. Why wouldn't she give him a break?

He wheeled around. "Stop it!" he said. To no one at all. Just a wide-open space of concrete and lawn, children and cyclists, a tower. Where was she? What was she doing? Where had she gone?

Oh. There. Way over there.

A willowy figure, impossibly tall, her hair as white as winter snow and her skin a deep brown. You couldn't miss her, even from here.

She was ignoring him, hands behind her back, staring up from the base of the tower to the very top.

She made her way to the public entrance, rummaging in the folds of that baggy thing she was wearing. For what? Coins? She never carried them. She wouldn't get in. They wouldn't let her. Not without paying. It wasn't allowed. Not even Pernille could spirit herself through a turnstile in daylight with all these people about.

He watched her dip her head and talk to the hazy face behind the glass of the ticket booth. Nodding, laughing, throwing her arms around happily. Dazzling them. She was dazzling them. Whoever was behind that glass was getting dazzled. He'd fallen for it himself a hundred times, and he still didn't know how. He resisted every time, but to no avail.

And then she was through, beyond the gate, waving goodbye to her brand new friend and disappearing into the base of the tower.

Frederik groaned out loud, put a hand to his head, and screwed his eyes shut. Anyone might be up there. People they needed to stay away from. Why was she always so reckless? They weren't safe yet. She *knew* that.

Just two months earlier, they had greatly disrupted a prominent public event. You never ever did that on Frederik's Hill. Ever. They had gone to the zoo with good intentions: to save the life of the mayor. But the mayor was not the role model everyone imagined. She had caused and then ruthlessly covered up an earthquake, and only Frederik and Pernille knew the truth. The mayor's detectives had almost caught them that night. An elephant had intervened, and a secret, underground train had swept them to safety. But were they out of the woods? No.

They'd lain low ever since. For more than two months.

Kept a low profile, stayed out of sight—and getting Pernille to stay out of sight was about as easy as hiding a lighthouse in a busy public street, a deception worthy of the mayor herself. The girl was like a beacon. You could see her from one hundred yards and hear her from three hundred—whether you wanted to or not. For Frederik, it was easy to pass unnoticed. He was short for his age and wholly unremarkable to look at. But Pernille Yasemin Jensen was as un-unremarkable as it got. She absolutely shouldn't go up that tower!

The top of it opened out to a viewing platform. People up there, of course. It was quite the attraction, especially on a sunny Saturday afternoon. He couldn't see her. Not yet. No mess of white hair among the others looking down at him.

Hold on.

Why were those others looking down at him?

The sun was bright, and he had to squint to figure out who it was.

Oh no!

And Pernille heading up there on her own!

He shielded the sun with the flat of a hand. Was he

right? Yes. Erica Engel, hateful. Frederik Dahl Dalby, worse. And Calamity Claus, calamitous.

And when Pernille reached the top of that tower, it would be more than calamity. It would be bad words and bitter battle and all in public. Not low profile at all!

So now he was jogging. Not going home. Not getting the downtime he had hoped for. That wasn't happening. Instead, he was running over the lawn to the base of the tower and thrusting some money at the face behind the glass. How much? *That* much? To climb a tower? Were they serious?

Into the cool of a gray-walled passage. A tiled floor spiraling upward. Splashes of light from the narrow windows as he puffed uphill. Glimpses through glass of the mall in the distance. Trees. The back of the library. The upper windows of apartment blocks. The orange slope of the roofs. Chimneys. Sky.

"Wait for me," he muttered. "Pernille, wait for me."

He was out of breath. His face was hot. His footsteps slapped on the tiles. A door to the open air. He stumbled outside. He stopped, panting, no idea which way he was pointing.

"Flipper-rack." Erica Engel, his nastiest of neighbors,

emerged from the blaze of sunlight, sneering. "You're here too? They *are* letting their standards slip."

Frederik Dahl Dalby slimed across the viewing platform, looking down his nose. "Your weird friend is over there. We were just advising her to go somewhere else. Dangerous places, towers. Accidents happen. Don't they, Calamity?"

Calamity Claus was the most accident-prone individual on Frederik's Hill. He was leaning over the railings, paying no attention to the dizzying vertical drop. He gave a knowing chuckle and nodded.

At the far side of the platform was Pernille, arms folded tight, one leg crossed in front of the other, eyes narrowed in anger.

What had they said to her? He could guess. *Weird. Freak. Foreigner.* Or worse.

Are you all right? he mouthed.

She shrugged. Looked away. Wouldn't give the bullies the satisfaction of knowing she wasn't.

Air and sky all around them. A jumble of rooftops and chimneys. The uppermost windows of Municipal Hall, a couple of streets away. At its corner, a tall lighthouse that nobody knew was a lighthouse, a balcony halfway up its side, a clock above that, reading a quarter past three. And at the very top, massive screens of glass facing out from a green copper lantern house. Another of the mayor's dark secrets. It made him shiver. Who did she spy on from up there? Or more to the point, who *didn't* she spy on?

"Nothing to say, Flabby-wreck?" Frederik Dahl Dalby said, breathing down his neck.

"*Don't* mock my accent."

"What do you expect?" Erica laughed. "You can't even say your own name properly."

It was true. Frederik was almost twelve and he'd lived here all his life, but he couldn't shake the traces of his parents' foreign accent. The local language was impossible. Nothing was pronounced the way it looked. *Pernille* rhymed with *vanilla, Claus* rhymed with *mouse*, and *Frederik* rhymed with nothing whatsoever. Was that his fault? No, it wasn't.

"I'll say my name however I like."

"Oooh! Look who's gotten all brave."

"Shut up."

"What are you going to do about it, Fiddle-rock?" Dahl Dalby said. "There are none of your imaginary *zombies* to protect you up here."

Frederik looked right into Dahl Dalby's eyes. "What did you say to Pernille?"

"Nothing she doesn't deserve."

"What does she deserve?" Frederik was getting angry. "Insults? And why? Because she's a tiny bit different from you?" He wasn't going to stand by and let them do this anymore. He'd scared them away once. He and Pernille. Trapped in the dark by a whole group of them. *Zombies*, he had shouted. *They're here for your souls*. And Frederik Dahl Dalby, Erica Engel, Calamity Claus, and the rest had fallen for it and fled like frightened lambs.

The memory made him smile.

"What?" said Dahl Dalby, instantly annoyed. "*What?*"

Erica Engel crowded in from the left. Pernille drifted their way. She'd seen he was outnumbered.

"Something to say to us, Feather-neck?" said Erica.

"No," Frederik sighed. He pushed between the bullies and headed for the railing. Calamity Claus watched him come, leaned back, and folded his arms in a way that was probably meant to seem threatening, lost his balance, and tipped over the railing, eyes wide, flailing for a handhold.

Frederik grabbed his hand and yanked him back to

the viewing platform. Calamity Claus fell hard on the stone, banged his knee, and yelped.

"You're welcome," Frederik said. He placed his hands on top of the railing and gazed into the distance, across the leafy trees of the Garden Park, up toward the summit of Frederik's Hill. Above the eighteenth-century castle, flags flapped in the breeze. The yellow stone was patterned with white-framed windows, sunlight splintering off the glass. Steep grass ramparts fell away from its toes to the boating lake below.

Beyond the castle, out of sight, hidden below a lawn so flat and featureless that no one ever asked, there was one more secret—an old secret. Older than the mayor. A rusting complex of water tanks, long forgotten. It fed a maze of pipes that wormed and twisted under the whole of the borough. Those pipes did not react well to water pressure anymore. And living very nearby was an addled elephant keeper who firmly believed there was something bad inside those pipes.

Zombies.

The bullying neighbors didn't scare Frederik anymore, but they were cruel and unkind. They'd hurt Pernille, and they deserved whatever he could think up.

"You're right about the zombies," he said. Softly.

"What?" said Dahl Dalby, close behind him.

"What?" asked Erica Engel.

"There are no zombies here," Frederik said.

"No kidding," Erica scoffed.

"They don't exist," said Dahl Dalby.

Frederik ignored them. Continued to stare at the castle on the hill. "The zombies are up there."

Dahl Dalby, Erica, and Calamity Claus must have managed a full twenty seconds before they looked. He could tell how hard they were trying not to, gathered at the railing, faces frozen, blinking too much.

Claus gave in. "Up where?"

"Up there." Frederik nodded toward the castle and the hill. "In their subterranean lair."

"What lair?"

"There is no lair."

"He's lying."

"He's a liar!"

"No, he isn't." Pernille had joined them so quietly they hadn't seen her arrive.

It made Erica jump, and that made her mad. She glared at Pernille. Bared her teeth. "Weirdo," she hissed.

"When the zombies come," said Frederik, "they will come from up there. They will sweep down the hillside, striking whoever crosses their path, crushing all before them."

"You're making it up."

"If only I were."

Dahl Dalby laughed. He tried to make it dismissive, disdainful. But it wasn't convincing. He stared with Erica and Claus across the gaping space of sunshine and rooftops, treetops and hillside. Each of them suddenly paled.

"Anyway," said Frederik. "See you around." He took Pernille's arm, and the two of them slipped through the door to the top of the ramp.

"Dimwits," said Pernille.

"Half-wits," said Frederik.

"And you duped them again, muffin. Thank you for that. Let's visit someone more friendly. Let's get ourselves some half-price chocolate."

"All right, Miss Adventure," he chuckled. "Let's do that."

Contagious

The two of them swung through the door of the Ramasubramanian Superstore. It was musty smelling and oddly warm, with refrigerators rattling like they wouldn't last the day.

"Zombies," Pernille laughed. "They fell for it completely. *Again.*"

"Young man and young lady of the special club!" exclaimed Venkatamahesh Ramasubramanian. "Welcome back! My first customers today." The little shopkeeper's face sagged—it was midafternoon, after all. His business never seemed to improve. He wasn't local enough for the

locals. But Frederik and Pernille shopped here whenever they could. Mr. Ramasubramanian had helped them during their escapades with the mayor back in the spring. They had made him an inaugural member of their club of outsiders and misfits.

"What can I offer you?" he said. "Cocoa? I have plenty of cocoa. Special offer!" He gestured at a mountain of cans of cocoa powder piled high and scraping the ceiling.

"But it's almost summer, dear man," Pernille said. "Cocoa? The sun is shining out there."

"Why have you got so much of it?" Frederik wondered.

"I invested in a bulk consignment," the shopkeeper said, all the more deflated. "To restock after the colossal kerfuffle of which we do not speak. There was a wholesale discount. Special concessions and a cash-back coupon, redeemable in writing once all stocks are sold, subject to availability. Conditions apply."

"Have you sold any?"

"None at all. Not one tin. How I wish I could escape this millstone of a business."

Pernille wrapped one long leg around the other and pirouetted slowly on the sticky floor. It was almost graceful.

But not. "Wrong time of year for cocoa," she said. "Could you disguise it as something more summery?"

"How about some kind of iced beverage?" Frederik said. "Call it *chococcino*. The big festival is soon. Think of all those thirsty people heading to the park. Thousands of them. They'll pass directly by your door. Mix up a vat of iced chococcino and you'll make a fortune."

Mr. Ramasubramanian's eyes brightened. "You are right. Why didn't I think of that?"

"It wouldn't occur to most minds," Pernille said. "But my friend and I are experts at the unexpected. We've been practicing. Ever since the... Well, you remember."

"The kerfuffle?" The little man stood before his unwanted cocoa and clasped his hands in nervous excitement. "Iced chococcino. I like that."

"Everyone will like it," said Frederik. "It's a guaranteed bestseller. Now, do you have any special offers for us? Pulverized popcorn? Squished jelly beans?"

"You are a businessman, young sir." Mr. Ramasubramanian waggled his head in respect. "A born persuader."

"And summoner of zombies," Pernille added, and they both laughed out loud.

"Zombies?" the shopkeeper said, taken aback.

"He set them on the neighbors," Pernille explained. "Frightened them silly. And not for the first time."

"That was *you*?"

"Imaginary zombies," Frederik clarified. "Obviously. Zombies don't exist."

"They don't?"

"No, of course not. We got the idea from a man we met some months ago. But he's insane. There's no such thing as zombies."

The shopkeeper eyed Frederik, doubtful. He stepped to the counter and a pile of unsold newspapers. "Yesterday's," he said, and held one up for them to see.

The headline hit Frederik like a punch to the stomach. "'Children Flee from Zombies'?" he gasped.

"Oh yes," Pernille said. "Hadn't you heard? It's trending all over the social."

"The what?"

"The social media. Don't you dabble? I've been liking and un-liking things all morning. It's hard to keep up. I've eleven thousand four hundred and sixty-three friends."

He looked her directly in the chin. She was quite a lot taller than him. "No, you haven't."

"But I have. It's so simple."

"Do you know who any of them are?"

"Is that important? I hardly think so."

He took the paper and stared at it, appalled.

"Zombies are a worrying development," Mr. Ramasubramanian said, "for a borough that prides itself on order."

"It's a joke. A mistake. A silly rumor."

Venkatamahesh rubbed at his forehead. "Vetala," he said. "I fear it is the vetala of Hindu mythology: malevolent spirits who seize control of the bodies of the dead. My mother would speak of them sometimes in a hushed tone. They haunt the charnel grounds. They drive people to terror and madness."

"It's madness for sure," said Frederik, "but I assure you it's all made up. By a madman. He's completely bananas."

"Who is he?" asked Venkatamahesh.

"No one you'd know," said Frederik and Pernille at exactly the same time.

"Forget I mentioned him," Frederik said.

"Nothing to worry about," Pernille added.

But it was. It really was.

Because there *had* been a colossal kerfuffle at the zoo after the earthquake, and while they hadn't exactly caused it, they had played a very visible role in it. For weeks after, they barely dared to go outside. But school was school, and they couldn't hide away. They had to carry on like normal—saying nothing, playing dumb.

It had, for once, been useful that other kids ignored them. Pernille was just that weird girl: too tall, too talkative, hair the wrong color for the rest of her. And Frederik was that short boy who couldn't pronounce his own name. They took to meeting in secret after school, in side streets and alleyways. Pernille would chat at a pace he couldn't process, he would try to reply, she would talk over him, and he would eventually stagger away, head buzzing. And oddly content. It was a rather extraordinary thing.

As the weeks passed, he'd finally started to feel safe again. Stopped looking over his shoulder. Stopped listening for that knock at the door. No one ever mentioned what had happened. The mayor's clampdown was comprehensive. She had a festival to prepare for, a reputation to protect, and frankly, that was great. Precisely what they needed. Everything back to normal, more or less.

But now, from nowhere, zombies! What possible explanation could there be for zombies? Only one. And it pointed ominously back to Frederik and Pernille.

They hit the street, passing Frederik's Sushi, Frederik's Hardware, and Frederik's Espresso. On Frederik's Hill, it didn't pay to name a business anything else. Pernille headed inside the upholsterer's workshop where she lived, and he carried on around the corner to his own house, a block away.

Mother wasn't home. Still at work at the library. He headed upstairs and found his father sitting in his office.

"Freddy!" said Father. "How's your Saturday?" He balanced his spectacles on top of his head, stretched in his chair, and nearly toppled backward. "Heard the news? Hilarious." He flipped his computer keyboard over and peeled a sticky note from the underside. "My password," he explained. He typed, and his face was bathed in light from the screen.

"That's not a secure place to keep your password."

"Don't worry. Get a load of this!"

"What is it? An email?" Frederik said. "To you?"

Immediate, it said. *From the Office of Her Ladyship the Mayor of Frederik's Hill. Kindly draft urgent resolution prohibiting all discussion of zombies, undead creatures, fanciful monsters of distressing nature, and zombies.*

"It says 'zombies' twice," Frederik said, his stomach fluttering.

"You've heard all this nonsense that's going about? The stories you kids are cooking up."

"Us kids?" Frederik said, and pretended to be calm about it. "Oh, yes. That? Yes."

"The way I hear it," Father chuckled, "you've all gone zombie bonkers! The zombie invasion of Frederik's Hill. Fantastic. The mayor, of course, is hopping mad about it. But she's always hopping mad about something. Pressures of the job, I suppose. In the Regulations Department, we're keeping our heads down and pretending it isn't funny."

"It isn't funny," Frederik said.

"It's hilarious. A hoot and a load of old hooey. Do you know where it came from? *I* do. I bet you can't guess."

Frederik tried to swallow the lump in his throat. Him. It came from him. Frederik. "I can't imagine," he managed.

"The editor of the *Frederik's Hill Times*! Thomas Dahl Dalby. He lives across the courtyard." Father nodded at the window and the golden afternoon beyond. "His son is your age. You must know the boy."

"Frederik," said Frederik coldly. "Frederik Dahl Dalby."

"That's him. One of your friends?"

"No."

"Wise. His dad is widely known as Bad News Tommy. But the Dahl Dalbys have it coming this time." His eyes twinkled with mischief. "Her Ladyship wants Dalby Senior drawn and quartered unless he names his source."

Frederik was nodding along, but he was having difficulty breathing properly.

"Thing is," Father went on, "Dalby Senior got the whole story from Dalby Junior. His son! The kid's convinced he was chased by a swarm of zombies. Is it a swarm? A plague? Well, anyway. There were a lot of them, according to the lad. And now the whole of Frederik's Hill is talking about it."

Frederik was nodding and nodding, couldn't bring his head to stop, didn't know what to do with it instead. "And when," he said, "is this supposed to have happened? This zombie thing?"

"That's the funniest part," said Father. "Apparently, it was ages ago. A couple of months. But the boy never said.

Just told his friends, a bunch of kids, and never mentioned a word to a grown-up. You can imagine what happened next." He leaned close. "It's gone bacterial."

"You mean viral?"

"Completely contagious. Brilliant, isn't it?" He rocked back in his chair with a belly laugh. "Serves the poisonous so-and-so right. Anyway. Better get on. Zombie embargo to enforce. No time for gossip. What would Her Ladyship say?" And he chuckled to himself while Frederik stared at his knees in shock. Frederik Dahl Dalby! Chased by zombies a couple of months ago. Frederik knew exactly when and exactly where and exactly who had brought those zombies to be. It was him and Pernille. Tired of the harassment, hitting back with a made-up story. *Zombies!* they had yelled to those kids in the dark. To Frederik Dahl Dalby. *Zombies are coming!*

And now, today, he'd done it again.

"By official decree of the borough of Frederik's Hill," his father mumbled, typing two-fingered, "the following supernatural beings are hereby banned from mention, conversation, communication, or other representation within the municipal boundaries originally designated by King Frederik the First."

He paused, intertwined his fingers, flexed them the wrong way, laughed out loud once more, and then resumed. "Zombies, all forms; undead creatures; walking dead; crawling dead; dead on skateboards, trolleys, bikes, or otherwise mobile by any mode or means. Also ghosts, spirits, manifestations, specters, spooks, and ghouls." He glanced sideways at Frederik and winked. "No point having this job if we can't have fun with it, is there?"

Frederik was too distracted to answer, heart racing. He'd spent sixty-something days under the radar. And while he was under the radar, staying out of conversations, feigning everything as normal, he had missed an epidemic of zombie rumors—a contagious epidemic that could be traced directly to him!

"You're not a fan of this Dahl Dalby kid?" Father asked.

"He's a bully. He's mean."

"Like father, like son. His dad's always pointing the finger at someone for something they didn't do. The mayor takes him seriously too. You feeling all right? You look a bit off."

"Not feeling great, no."

"Have a lie-down."

"I think I should."

"I think you should."

Frederik wandered, listless and queasy, out of the office and up the stairs.

Father called after him, "Who will the evil Dahl Dalbys blame for this zombie malarkey, I wonder?"

"I wonder," Frederik echoed, chilled to the stomach and heading to his room to hide.

Pa-pah

Early next morning, Frederik slipped along the front of the upholsterer's shop and pressed his nose to the dew on the glass. Should he knock?

Over his shoulder, across the street, café proprietor Gretchen Grondal was outside her café with a notebook and pencil, watching anything and anyone that moved. That was bad. Very bad. He'd stayed out of her sight for weeks, ever since the chaos at the zoo. Miss Grondal had been a principal casualty, knocked out cold for more than a day. That hadn't been their fault either, but Miss Grondal was unlikely to care. She could identify Frederik and Pernille. Name them. Blame them.

Nevertheless, he *had* to risk being seen. *Had* to reach Pernille. If the Dahl Dalbys talked, they'd be named and blamed for sure. He knocked on the glass. Knocked *loud.*

The shop was a ramshackle building in salmon-pink plaster, a tile roof folded over the upstairs like an enormous, sat-upon hat. He had never been inside. The ground floor was split by a passageway leading to a courtyard behind. To its left was a showroom, tidy and refined. A sofa in pink-and-white stripes sat proudly in the window, books of fabrics on a table, everything in its place. To the right of the passageway, anarchy. Three chaotic workshops opened onto one another. Furniture and tools and pieces of wood and fabric everywhere.

A shadow appeared at the back of the workshop. A tall figure at the foot of narrow stairs. But not Pernille: a long, lean, fully grown man. The man flapped a hand in irritation, waving Frederik away.

Frederik knocked again, mouthing a plea.

The man shook his head and motioned him away again.

Frederik dared a third time. The man strode across the unlit workshop, angrily rattled the bolts, and tugged the door open. He was bearded and blond. He seemed a hundred feet tall.

"Shut!" he shouted, despite being very nearby indeed. Frederik was forced to step back and look up.

"Sunday!" the man insisted. "We are shut!"

"Yes," said Frederik, collecting himself. "The thing is—"

"Shut! Tell your mother we are shut!"

"My mother?"

"Closed!"

"Why my mother?"

"Whoever sent you. Who sent you?"

"Nobody sent me."

"*Nobody* sent you?" The giant man seemed all the more outraged. "*Nobody?*"

"I came of my own accord," said Frederik, his courage collapsing.

"On a Sunday? A boy?" The man stepped clean out of the door and forced Frederik toward the bicycle lane. A boy could be killed in the bicycle lane. Those cyclists stopped for no one. Straying into a bicycle lane was suicide. Forcing a boy into one was attempted murder! The attempted murderer looked clear over Frederik's head and gave a little wave. Frederik turned to see Miss Grondal staring, as severe as ever.

"What," the attempted murderer demanded, "could

a boy of... What are you, anyway? Eleven or something? What could a boy of eleven or something possibly need of his own accord on a Sunday? Rip your mother's sofa, did you? Need an urgent repair before she gets home? Hmm?"

"No. I'm here to see Pernille."

"Pernille?" said the man.

"Pernille. A girl. Tall. White hair. She lives here, I believe. Somewhere. Upstairs. I'm not really sure."

"You're here to see Pernille? Of your own *accord*?"

"Yes."

"You're a boy." The man doubled forward and thrust his face uncomfortably close. "A *boy*!"

"That is correct, yes. Would you happen to know where I could find her?"

"Depends," said the man. He put his hands in his pockets. He gazed toward the café and attempted to smooth his tufty hair with a giant hand.

"What might it depend on, please?" Frederik asked.

The man rubbed his beard. "Screening."

"Screening?"

"The girl in question," the man said, "is my adopted daughter. I am her adoptive papa." He pronounced it as she would: Pa-pah. "Her lawful guardian. It is my job to guard her." He regarded Frederik closely. He had long, fair eyelashes and deep blue eyes. "Are you selling something?"

"No," said Frederik.

"Are you buying something?"

"No."

"Are you hoping to ask her out on a date?"

"No! No, no."

"Why not? What's wrong with her?"

There were a great many things wrong with her, but it didn't seem the moment to say so. Frederik considered going home. But nonexistent zombies had raised their undead heads, and he needed to warn Pernille.

"I just want to tell her something. Is she home?"

"Come with me." And Frederik was grabbed by the collar and hauled rather roughly up the step into the gloom of the workshop.

There was a workbench with a settee on it. Enormous pins in rows in the fabric. Drills and staple guns hanging from nails in the wall. Cans piled on racks, scissors and hammers and chisels and pliers, glues in pots, yarns in knots. An army of bobbins pinned to a board, threads of every color. Scraps of fabric everywhere, in piles, all over the floor. Sewing machines and rulers and tape measures, things on hooks, things on chairs, chairs on top of other chairs, and barely room to move.

Pernille's papa strode to the foot of the narrow staircase. "Pernille?" he yelled.

There was no reply.

"Pernille?"

Nothing happened.

"Perhaps," said Frederik, edging toward the door, "I chose a bad moment."

"Oh yes," said her papa. "Without a doubt."

"Oh. Perhaps I should come back at a more convenient time?"

"She's thirteen," her papa explained. "You would need to wait approximately seven years for a convenient time. Pernille?" he yelled again. "A young man is here. He wishes to tell you something."

Somewhere overhead, a floorboard creaked. Somewhere up the stairs, a light turned on.

"A young man with flowers," her papa called out. "Roses. Red."

Roses? Frederik had not brought roses. Should he have brought roses? He wasn't sure. He had never called on her before. Or anyone else, come to that.

"Go away!" Shrill defiance from somewhere up those stairs. "Leave me alone!"

"Better put them in water. They'll wilt."

This was going entirely wrong. Frederik turned to leave, but not in time. With a huff and a flounce, Pernille appeared in the stairwell.

"Which young man?" she demanded to know. "What roses?"

"This young man."

She stepped into the workshop. "Little muffin!" she said. "What a lovely surprise. Where are my flowers?"

Frederik looked at Pernille's papa. Pernille's papa looked at Frederik, frowned, and said, "Yes, young man. Where are my daughter's flowers?"

Frederik's mouth opened and closed, somewhat like a haddock.

Pernille scowled and swiped at her papa's arm, extremely hard. He barely seemed to notice. "There are no flowers," she exclaimed. "You horrible, horrible, horrible,

horrible man." And she punctuated each *horrible* with a punch to her lawful guardian's bicep.

"No," Frederik said. "I just came to see you about, you know, the *zombies*."

"The what?" said her papa.

Frederik tried to signal to Pernille with his eyes. "Could we just speak in private for a moment?"

"Certainly not," said her papa. "Not without a guardian guarding."

Pernille sighed.

Her papa scratched his head and peered out the huge front window. "Let's head across the street to Café Grondal and chat over brunch among the borough's elite. What do you think? Are we too shabby?"

"Without doubt," said Pernille.

"Perfect. That'll get right up their snooty noses, I expect."

"We can't go over there," said Frederik, panicking. "Miss Grondal was at the zoo! With the mayor!"

Pernille's papa gave a hearty laugh. "I heard that story."

"You *heard*?"

"Not from me," Pernille assured him hurriedly.

"I heard it from Miss Grondal herself. From the horse's

mouth. Would we describe her as a horse? Graceful and equine? Maybe not. More like a funny, fussy bird."

"Or a vulture," Frederik said.

"That's unkind." The upholsterer frowned. "Miss Grondal can seem stern, but I don't buy it. Underneath, there's a fluffy little chickadee yearning to fly free."

Pernille glared at him. "Have you been flirting with her? I told you not to flirt with her. She's mean and spiteful."

"Fluffy," he told her. "Chickadee. Underneath. She and I have an understanding. I buy coffee, lend an ear. She tells me things—who's in the market for furniture, who needs a repair. She refers her customers to me, and I send mine to her. That's business, how the world goes around. And sometimes there are, you know, little confidences."

Pernille gasped, appalled. "Such as?"

"Well, her zoo story, for starters. Miss Grondal, it seems, one evening not long ago, went to the zoo. Some society event. Bigwigs, hobnobbing. She remembers arriving, taking a seat, and having a glass of wine."

"And then?" Frederik was cold all over. Was their secret out?

"And then she woke up at home in an armchair,

still in her fancy clothes, at dawn. But it wasn't the next morning. It was the day after that! And she has no memory of anything in between. Absolute blank. Must have been a big glass of wine."

Frederik blinked. Twice. "She has no memory at all?"

"On my honor as a member of the Royal Order of Upholsterers."

"*Are* you a member?" Pernille checked.

"More or less." He gazed out across the street. "Come on," he said. "Coffee. Can't function without it. Miss Grondal's fault. She's got me hooked."

"No, no," said Frederik. "Let's stay here. I only need a minute."

"I think we can risk it," Pernille said. "Sounds like Miss Grondal has a case of amnesia."

"No. Wait."

But no one was waiting. Pernille's papa was out the door and heading briskly away. Pernille followed.

"Wait!" he called after her. "We can't go there! We'll be *recognized*."

"Don't worry," her papa called back. "There's no one at Café Grondal who'd have any interest in you."

A Vulture

"Come back," he attempted, but was drowned out by traffic. Pernille and her papa were already across the street, almost at the café. And in the doorway, watching them come, stood Gretchen Grondal. Face pinched. Hair swept back in the strictest knot. Apron, notepad, pencil. Ready to record the slightest infraction. She had seen Frederik. She looked directly at him. Had she recognized him? Did she remember? Surely she couldn't possibly have forgotten the night at the zoo?

There was a row of tables outside the café's front

window. Well-dressed adults sipped coffee piled high with cream. Pernille and her papa helped themselves to a table. Frederik came puffing up to them. "Pernille! We shouldn't be here."

"Nonsense," said her papa. "We are as entitled to be here as any of these hoity-toity townsfolk." He said it loud enough for all of them to hear and flashed a winning smile at a lady in a shawl at a nearby table. "Now," he announced, fixing his attention on Frederik. "What is this fabulous secret you need to tell us?"

Frederik could hardly breathe. This was *such* a bad idea. Gretchen Grondal was heading their way, sizing them up with mean little eyes, extending her talons.

"Miss Grondal!" Pernille's papa exclaimed. "You are more radiant than the morning sun this Sunday. Did you get your hair done?"

"No," she said, startled.

"Excellent!" And he smiled with roughly one hundred gleaming teeth. "Such striking eyes you have. Aquamarine. I have a ream of fabric exactly that shade. I'm saving it for the right someone."

Miss Grondal's eyes opened wider. They were watery

gray, not aquamarine at all. They narrowed again with suspicion. "Would you care to order?"

"Coffee!" Pernille's papa demanded. "Enormous! Frothy and fantastic." He leaned toward her. "You know how I like it."

Miss Grondal's eyes swept Frederik's way. Locked on his. He held his breath and tried to shrink into his collar. Her forehead creased. "Do I know you?" she said.

"No," he croaked.

There was a long silence. Miss Grondal seemed to wrestle with a thought, and then to shake it off. Frederik's heartbeat thundered in his throat.

"Something to eat or drink?"

"Me?" he said. "No, thank you. No, I ought to be going, in fact."

"Sit down!" Pernille's papa pressed Frederik into the seat. "Have something now that you're here. Milk? Pop? Cake?"

"Ooh, cake," Pernille said, and Miss Grondal pivoted to her. Again, there was a spark of recognition that faded into confusion.

"Milk!" said Frederik, anxious to distract her. "No! Changed my mind. Cake." And all eyes were on him again.

"Cake." Miss Grondal scratched a note. Her every gesture was spiteful.

"Make it three," said Pernille's papa, oblivious. "Walnut. On one of those plates. With the lacy doily." And he winked at Miss Grondal.

"*Stop* it!" Pernille hissed as Miss Grondal stalked away. "You're *flirting*. With the enemy!"

"Flirting? Me?"

"Flirting!"

He stretched back in his chair, and his long legs rocked the table. "What makes poor Gretchen anyone's enemy? She makes me coffee. Extremely good coffee. Foamy. Great big piles of creamy foam on it. Wonderful."

"She's in cahoots with the mayor," Frederik told him. "She's the official caterer for the mayor's Midsummer Festival!" And he opened his eyes wide to signal just how serious that was.

Pernille's papa, unaware of the mayor's misdeeds like almost everyone, didn't get it. "Well, that's nice, then." He settled his hands behind his head and basked in what little sunshine filtered through the clouds. He glanced sideways at Pernille. "She'd make a fine mama, don't you think?"

Pernille nearly popped. "*What?* No! Gretchen Grondal? Are you out of your mind?"

Her papa shrugged. "You keep saying you want me to find you a mama."

"Not just *any* mama," she wailed. "My mama. My *real* mama!"

"We don't know who she was. I've told you that."

The upholsterer had adopted Pernille long ago. She remembered nothing about it. No details of her birth parents were known, but she had a burning urge to find them—her mother in particular. For years, she had believed her to be Her Ladyship the Mayor—a sad mistake the mayor had cruelly crushed when they finally met.

"Miss Grondal!" the upholsterer declared. "You're back already. Is that my coffee? I do declare it's frothier than ever. It is your personal best. A world record. It is a monument in froth. An artwork. And you, mademoiselle, are a world champion foamy froth artiste."

Pernille clutched her head in her hands and groaned out loud.

The cup was placed before the upholsterer, with its mound of trembling foam. He caught Miss Grondal's cuff and said, "I hear you're to be the caterer for the mayor's Midsummer Festival. How prestigious! Tell me how you landed such a commission. Did you dazzle? Were you magnificent?"

Frederik's throat constricted completely. She'd won the commission that night at the zoo, and that was the very last thing they wanted her to think about.

"Well," Miss Grondal said, and her face clouded. "To tell you the truth, I can't entirely remember."

"You can't?" Frederik said.

She reddened. "It *is* official! I received a letter of confirmation. I signed a contract."

"Quite right," said Pernille's papa.

"But I don't recall exactly how I won it." She bent her head closer to the upholsterer and lowered her voice. "I think it was *that* evening. The one I told you about."

"Was it? The evening that slipped away? I see. Well, the deal is done, it seems, and you will be the toast of the town, no matter how it happened."

"Indeed I will."

A slice of walnut cake slid in front of Frederik, but he had no appetite at all, with Gretchen Grondal so close he could smell her sour lavender scent and with the night they dare not mention under discussion.

"I shall have to dress better when I call in the future," the upholsterer said.

Pernille placed a fingertip in her open mouth and made a gagging noise.

"What was that?" Miss Grondal snapped.

"Pernille," her papa murmured. "A little respect, please."

"Respect?" It seemed to pop out of Pernille by surprise. Her tone tilted.

Frederik found himself grabbing for cake he didn't want. It was all he could think of. "Yum!" he exclaimed, stuffing it in so fast he could no longer speak. "Delicious." Crumbs flew everywhere.

Pernille stared icily at Miss Grondal, and Miss Grondal stared icily back.

"I apologize," the upholsterer said. "I don't know what's gotten into my daughter today."

"No," said Miss Grondal. "Well. I expect it's that temperament, isn't it. She's of a different *nationality*, after all. You know. By birth."

"Nationality?"

"That's not what she means!" And Pernille was getting to her feet, tipping the table. A knob of foam fell off her papa's coffee into the saucer.

"At her age," Miss Grondal said, "a girl needs a female influence. A mother figure."

"She does!" said her papa, brightening. "My thoughts exactly."

"I," Pernille said, teeth gritted, fingertips gouging the tablecloth, "already. Have. A. Mother."

"Where?" Miss Grondal tipped her head.

"Gone, sadly," said her papa. "We don't know where. But there must be others who could play that role. Don't you think, Pernille? People close by? It's hard for busy businesspeople to find time for a family. But here we are, Miss Grondal and I, two businesspeople living so close together. I was simply thinking that between us we could—"

"No!" Pernille leapt up, the coffee flew sideways and clean off the edge of the table. It hit the concrete with a smash, and Frederik's ankles were instantly warm and damp. "I *have* a mama!" she shouted.

The other customers peered at her over their cups. A baby began to cry.

Gretchen Grondal stared intently at Pernille, head tilted, lips pursed. "You remind me of someone," she muttered.

"No, she doesn't," Frederik said.

"No, I don't," Pernille snapped. "I'm nothing to do with you!"

"Pernille, please." Her papa was reaching for her arm, but she shrugged him off. She forced her way out from behind the table, kicking a chunk of broken saucer into the street.

"Pernille!" Her papa was cross now, worried too. His calm and charm had disappeared.

"She is not my mama!" Pernille wheeled away, hair flying, skirts lashing, arms folded, head down. She marched away, along the street, toward Municipal Hall and the lighthouse that no one knew was there. She broke into a trot, and then a run.

"Wait! Pernille!" Her papa tried to go after her, but Miss Grondal caught his arm.

"Let her go," she told him. "She's a hothead, that one. It's the foreign blood."

"I'll go," Frederik said. "I'll catch up with her."

"Make sure she's all right," her papa called after him.

Frederik was far behind her. She had longer legs. She was past the duck pond already. Almost at the corner and the Ramasubramanian Superstore. Well, that was a safe place. He'd catch up with her there. Calm her down. They shouldn't have gone near Café Grondal. He knew they shouldn't. He'd said so. *Don't go there,* he'd said. They *had* to be more careful. And he still hadn't told her about the Dahl Dalbys and the zombies.

"Pernille!" he called, and ran as fast as he could.

A Foreign Person

Frederik veered through the door of the Ramasubramanian Superstore and pulled up sharp.

No one there.

"Hello? Pernille?"

No heads above the rickety racks. No one perusing the out-of-date produce. No Pernille. Where had she gone?

At the back of the store, beyond the counter, Venkatamahesh Ramasubramanian emerged from a darkened doorway. "Young businessman! You are back. I was just experimenting with the icy chocolate drink you inspired."

"Is Pernille here?" Frederik asked. "Have you seen her?"

"The extraordinarily tall young lady with the striking hair?"

"Yes, her."

"No."

"Rats!"

"But I wish she were here. She brightens my day. Such a vivacious young woman."

"We're in enormous trouble, you see. We made up those zombies, and now it's backfired."

"Such spirit. My mother would have told us—"

"Thanks then. Got to go."

"My *mother* would have told us," Venkatamahesh raised his voice, "that your friend reflects the auspicious qualities of a Lakshmi, wife of Shiva. Or was that Parvati? I really should have paid closer attention. Anyway, she would have said—"

"I really have to go!"

"Or was it Vishnu?"

"Thanks, then. See you." And Frederik made it out the door. Spotted two tall figures crossing the street. And then he made it back in the door, backward, at high speed, and threw himself headlong under a shelf.

The shopkeeper stared down at him from not very far up. "I recall there was one with a lot of arms," he said.

"Hide me!" Frederik hissed.

Thick, blue detergent dripped from dusty bottles onto the tile.

Two more people entered the store. Two huge men. In suits. Short hair and cold expressions. They examined Venkatamahesh's stock, while Frederik rolled himself farther under the rack. The shopkeeper clearly had no idea who they were. But Frederik knew. The mayor's detectives: Mortensen and Martensen.

"Welcome, gentlemen—welcome to the Ramasubramanian Superstore. Excellent goods at excellent prices, and open on Sundays for your extra convenience." Venkatamahesh gave a little laugh, giddy at receiving so many customers at once.

The two men did not laugh.

"Sundays," said one of them without emotion. He reached into a pocket, withdrew a notebook and a tiny ballpoint pen. He wrote something down. "Open," he repeated, "on Sundays."

His companion took a step closer to Venkatamahesh, staring down at him from a great height. "Are you aware, sir, of the borough's designated opening hours for retailers?"

"Yes," said Venkatamahesh. "Yes, I am. They are unnecessarily restrictive. Bad for business, and bad for you, my clientele." He smiled. "So I ignore them."

"'I...ignore...them,'" said the first man, writing that down as well.

"Lucky for you! So, as the only grocer open today, can I interest you in some groceries? Cocoa powder? Buy two get one free. Or..." His face lit up. "Would you care to sample an experimental iced concoction? A recently invented, soon-to-be-patented Midsummer Festival souvenir."

One of the detectives squinted. "Souvenir?"

"Exclusive limited edition for festival goers. Be the first to try the prototype. Half off."

"The caterer for the festival," the detective said, "is the Café Grondal. Souvenirs are subject to license."

"License?"

"Got one?"

"Erm..."

"You don't. I know that for a fact, Mr.... What is your name, sir?"

"Ramasubramanian."

The detective with the pen blinked blankly at his pad.

Then at Venkatamahesh. Started writing. Slowly. “Llama,” he said, “submarine.”

His partner walked around Venkatamahesh in a tight loop. His shiny shoes passed just inches in front of Frederik’s nose. “Submarine, sir?”

“No. Not a submarine.”

“You’re denying it now?”

“Denying what?” Venkatamahesh was becoming anxious.

“Why,” said the first, “would a keeper of a convenience store several miles from the sea have need of a *submarine,* Mr. Llama?”

“My name is not Llama.”

“You gave a false name?”

“Who are you? Why are you asking me these questions?”

“Why are you avoiding them? Why do you keep changing your answers? What are you hiding, Mr. so-called Llama? And where is your submarine? Are you a subaquatic smuggler? A spy? You’re not from hereabouts, would that be correct? Where are you from, sir? Somewhere foreign? Are you a *foreign* person, Mr. Llama? Where are Llamas from, exactly, sir?”

“The Andes,” said the other detective.

"Are you from the Andes, Mr. Llama? Or is *Llama* an alias? A devious pseudonym? Are you, in fact, *not* from the Andes at all?"

Frederik's head was wedged at an awkward angle underneath the shelf. There was grime and gooey liquid on the floor. He could smell it. His arm was going to sleep. But he couldn't move. Didn't dare. He'd be heard, seen, recognized instantly. These were the same detectives he and Pernille had eluded that night at the zoo. Now he was trapped. Couldn't escape. Couldn't help Mr. Ramasubramanian, couldn't find Pernille, couldn't move.

"I want you to leave my shop," Venkatamahesh said, shaken. "Leave, or I will call the police."

One of the detectives produced a card. Held it up for Venkatamahesh to read.

"Oh," said Venkatamahesh. "You are the police."

"Your submarine," the detective growled.

"I do not have a submarine."

"*Denies,*" the second one wrote, "owning…aforementioned…submarine."

"I have never *seen* a submarine!"

"And what, Mr. Llama, do you carry in your

suddenly nonexistent submersible? Hmm? Might it be"—and he paused for an excruciatingly long intake of breath—"zombies?"

Involuntarily, Frederik's head jerked up. Smacked the underside of the shelf. Metal rattled. A bottle of laundry detergent skipped an inch in the air and landed with a thud. Frederik gave a hiss of pain. His vision went all wrong.

Two pairs of shiny shoes turned his direction, squeaking on the sticky linoleum. "What was that?" a detective asked somewhere far above.

Frederik held his breath, eyes watering. Any moment, they were going to crouch down and look under the shelf and straight into his eyes.

"Oh, that little noise?" Venkatamahesh replied hurriedly. "It felt like a tremor, don't you think?"

"Tremor?"

No! Frederik mouthed, willing Venkatamahesh to stop.

"An earthquake!" the shopkeeper said. "Oh no. Please move toward the door in accordance with borough evacuation regulations." There was hesitation. Murmuring. But on Frederik's Hill, rules were rules. Two pairs of shiny shoes and one pair of shabby slippers moved away, toward the daylight, leaving Frederik behind. Venkatamahesh had covered for him. But at what cost?

"Earthquake?" a detective said, very doubtful indeed.

"Just like before. Remember?"

"There was no earthquake," Venkatamahesh was told in a menacing tone.

Frederik wriggled and peered out from under the cornflakes.

"There was," said Venkatamahesh. "You must remember it, surely? My mother would have told us it was the deity Ganesh, Remover of Obstacles." He glanced around his shabby store. "I wish he'd remove mine."

"Deity?" a detective asked, uncertain.

"Ganesh is the one with the head of an elephant," Venkatamahesh explained.

"Elephant?" the detective said. "You know about that?"

"No!" Frederik breathed. "No, no, no."

"I surmise," said Venkatamahesh.

"You *surmise* the shaking was caused by an elephant?"

"I'm speculating." Venkatamahesh was sounding ever more guilty.

"Have you mentioned this elephant to anyone, Mr. Llama?"

"No."

"Has someone mentioned it to you?"

"No."

One of them moved extremely close, forcing Venkatamahesh back to the refrigerator. "And did you speculate about zombies too?"

"Zombies? No. They were in the news."

"How did they get in the news, sir? Who mentioned them? Where did the story start?"

Venkatamehesh coughed. "Well, there is a legend—well, a fable, really. Well, a story. About the vetala. Not zombies, exactly. Well, similar. Dead, you see. Except alive. And walking around. They harass innocent people."

The detectives did that too. Heart thumping, Frederik quietly slithered sideways out from under the shelf, into the farthest aisle, head down. He crept to the rear of the store, the counter, the darkened doorway. Mortensen and Martensen weren't looking. They were focused on Venkatamahesh, who was gripping the edge of the fridge in fear. Frederik tried to catch his eye, to signal, but he couldn't.

"And where would you *speculate* these zombies are to be found, Mr. Llama?"

"Charnel grounds," the shopkeeper croaked.

"What exactly is a charnel ground?"

"Where corpses are left," he managed. "To decompose."

"Corpses?"

"Dead ones. It is a ritual."

"Ritual?"

"Yes."

"Corpses?"

"Yes."

"Zombies?"

"Yes. No."

"It's time we took a walk across the street, Mr. Llama."

"Oh. You're going?" Venkatamahesh's head lifted. "Good. All right then. Thank you for stopping by. I'm sorry I couldn't help you more. Safe journey."

"You don't understand." And they crowded him more, till he was all but sitting on top of the soda. "We are *all* taking a walk."

"All of us?"

"All of us."

"Me?"

"You."

"Where to?"

"To the mayor, Mr. Llama. Across the street, to Municipal Hall, to have a conversation with Her Ladyship the Mayor. About your story, sir. About your secret submarine. About your zombies."

"The mayor?"

"The mayor. And if I were someone like you, I would get my story straight."

Before Frederik could do a thing about it, Venkatamahesh was ushered out the door, onto the street, not even allowed to pause to lock up. And they were gone. All of them. For a walk.

To the mayor.

Frederik stood alone behind the counter. The fridge rattled unhealthily, and then the Ramasubramanian Superstore fell horribly silent.

Zombies

Branches whipped in the breeze and clattered windows. Birds were flung backward and sideways, litter lashed Frederik's ankles as he ran.

What had he done? He'd invented zombies to frighten bullies, and now the zombies had come alive. They were prowling the borough, out of control. Why hadn't he kept his big mouth shut? Venkatamahesh was in front of the mayor, facing her angry questions, ugly threats, lights shining in his eyes. He'd crack. He'd break, no matter how bravely he'd covered for Frederik back there. And where was Pernille? Where had she gone? Had they taken her too?

He galloped into the square. The mall was closed. The library too, its big glass doors locked and darkened.

"Pernille?" he shouted, and her name echoed around the fronts of the stern, empty buildings.

"Behind you," she called.

He whipped around, tripped, tumbled onto concrete.

She was sitting on a planter, tucked behind a wall. He had run straight by without seeing her.

"Venkatamahesh," he wheezed, clambering to his feet. "They got him. They took him. He's been taken. It's our fault. The zombies. They know about the zombies."

She took a long length of white hair and coiled it around her finger. "There are no zombies," she said. "Really. I don't have time for this today."

"You don't have *time*?" Frederik nearly exploded. "He's been taken away! He's been arrested. We got him arrested."

At that, her eyelids raised, and she unraveled her long, long legs. "And you're sure about this?"

"I was there! I was under a shelf."

"Were you? How odd."

"I was hiding. He hid me. He had to. No! He *didn't* have to. He could have given me away, but he hid me instead.

And then I let him get arrested! What have I done? They'll torture him. They'll get our names. They think he has a submarine."

"Has he?"

"No!"

"Pity. Well, I'll try to help where I can, but I have a lot on my plate."

"Like what?" He checked the street to make sure no one had followed him from the store.

"Finding my mama." She didn't say it exactly. She sort of sighed it. Breathed it out in a wave of longing.

"Oh," he said. "Right." Pernille's search for her real mama was familiar ground and he knew to tread it carefully. "Miss Grondal is twisted and mean. Ignore everything she said."

She let go of the curl of hair and it bobbed in midair like a spring. "Perhaps it's the wake-up I needed. I haven't been concentrating. I've neglected my search. I'm going to find her."

"Yes, you should. But first, can we please go somewhere safe?"

"Today."

"Today?"

"Today, muffin. I'm going to find my real mama today. I've been blind. I've been lax. I've been fast asleep at the wheel of fortune. How could I? What kind of daughter am I?"

"Pernille, this might not be the best time."

"What better time could there be? Right now. This moment. This day, this place. She's near. I know it. I feel her presence. I've always felt it. She's someone I know; I know she is. I must find her. No more delay. I won't have that harpy Gretchen Grondal pawing my papa!"

"All right. But let's get out of sight."

"No. I won't hide anymore."

He thought his head might burst. He scanned the surrounding streets again. He had to get her out of there. He had to get both of them out of there and fast. "*She's* hiding," he said. "Your mama is hiding. She must be. She's somewhere out of sight. Or you would have found her sooner."

Her eyes widened. "That's true. That's a good point."

"Come on!" He grabbed her hand and hauled her to her feet. A gust of wind bowled paper and dust across the wide-open square. They were terribly exposed. Might be seen from any angle. Where could they go?

"We know my mama is not the mayor," Pernille went on. "That childish illusion is behind me now. And she certainly isn't Gretchen Grondal. So who? Who is she? She'd be someone a lot like me, don't you think? Someone like us."

"A hopeless misfit hiding from the authorities?" he muttered.

"Yes. Perhaps that's it." She stared at the sky.

"We must go!"

She stared at the floor. "Someone who doesn't fit in. That must be right. Someone who cannot reveal herself." She stared across the square to the steps that led down to Frederik's Hill Central Railway Station. Blinked. Twice. "Surely not?" she whispered.

"Surely not what?"

"Surely not her?"

"Who?"

She grabbed his arm, and now it was she who was doing the hauling and he who was being hauled.

"Where are we going?"

"Out of sight," she said. "That's what you want, isn't it? Somewhere hidden."

"The train station?" he said as they reached the top of the steps.

"Exactly."

They plunged down the steep stairs to the station platform. It was quiet down there, but not for long. Within minutes, the whispery silence was shattered by a roaring diesel engine and the screech of ancient brakes. *Not In Service* said the sign. *Do Not Board.* But Frederik and Pernille knew this battered, blue train. They'd ridden it once by mistake, and another time by luck. This was how they'd escaped the mayor and her detectives.

The coaches were dilapidated, decades out-of-date. The doors burst open like weapons. No one ever boarded this train, though it looped the borough every half hour. No one apart from them.

He followed Pernille up the step and down the narrow aisle of the carriage, among threadbare seats long neglected, little lamps at tables set in the wall. The train growled out of the station, into darkness, daylight, and darkness again. There was a lurch, and he pitched forward, almost falling, and grabbed Pernille's arm.

"Bend the knees! Roll with the motion of the train."

The train conductor marched toward them from nowhere, hat askew and gaze askew-er. "Or simply sit down. It's safer. And while you're there, I'll take a look at your tickets please."

"We don't have tickets," Frederik managed.

"Relax, dear. I'm joking."

It was impossible to buy tickets for this train, as they knew. It only continued to run due to a bureaucratic oversight. And for all her official sternness, the conductor had helped them immensely in the past. In fact, it was she who had first suggested their club for outsiders. She gave an unexpected cackle, a glint in her eyes, one pointing a slightly different direction than the other. "I imagine if you two are back on my train, there must be a very good reason. Am I right? Sit down! Sit down! There's a really bumpy bit coming up any second."

Pernille did as she was told. That was unusual. The conductor took the opposite seat, and just in time. The carriage rocked and rattled madly and Frederik tumbled onto the rough upholstery. The conductor's graying hair was short beneath a battered, blue hat with the crest of Frederik's Hill. There were shiny patches at the elbows and cuffs of her blazer. Her skirt looked a little too worn. Everything about this train was worn: an underground branch line entirely forgotten by everyone up above.

Brakes whined, and the train slowed into the glow of another underground station. *Municipal Hall and Lighthouse.* Disused for years, by order of Her Ladyship the Mayor. Dust drifted along the platform. Frederik's breath caught. Somewhere directly above them, inside Municipal Hall, Venkatamahesh was facing the mayor. She'd make him talk. Name names. *Their* names: Frederik Sandwich. Pernille Yasemin Jensen. Wanted. For crimes against the borough. And guilty as could be.

"We *are* here for a reason," Pernille told the conductor.

"I knew it," said the conductor. "I could tell straightaway. You're not yourself."

"Am I not?" Pernille replied. "I don't know if I am. I don't know *who* I am. Never have." She raised her enormous eyes toward the conductor.

The conductor sighed. "You will, dear. Soon enough." And she leaned across the gap to give Pernille's knee a friendly rub.

Emotions leaked across Pernille's face, one after another—hope, excitement, worry.

"You think it's her?" Frederik realized.

"I think it's her," Pernille whispered.

"No," he said. "Pernille, no. I doubt that."

"Is it you?" She grabbed the conductor's hand. "What is your name?"

"*My* name, dear?" The conductor laughed. "How odd. It's usually my job to ask that question. My name is Edna. Edna Brink. And I'm delighted to see you both again, tickets or no tickets."

"Pernille Brink," said Pernille under her breath.

"No dear, Edna Brink."

"Please ignore my friend," Frederik interrupted. "There's been a misunderstanding."

"No, there hasn't," Pernille said.

Edna the conductor squinted at them both. "I think there might have been. I'm not following this conversation at all. Age, perhaps. Or too many loops of this branch line on my own. I fear I've gone loopy."

The train was moving again, Municipal Hall was slipping away into darkness. There was no way to get to Venkatamahesh. No way to help him.

Unless...

Frederik gulped. Edna the conductor? She had helped

them before. She'd warned them about the mayor. She knew the borough's secrets. And there was no one else.

"We're in trouble," he said. "Again."

"I thought so. What is it this time?"

"Zombies."

Her eyes scrunched up.

"The mayor is having people arrested. It's our fault. We mentioned the zombies. But zombies don't exist. How could they?"

"*Which* zombies, dear?"

"The ones the elephant keeper told us about."

"Rasmus?" she said, suddenly breathless. "Rasmus Rasmussen?" She had a lifelong crush on the elephant keeper, though she hadn't seen him for years.

"Yes. Rasmus thinks there are zombies. Here in these tunnels. He's out of his mind, of course. Completely doolally."

Worry descended on Edna. Her face became gray. "And you mentioned these zombies? Publicly?"

"Just to some kids. What's wrong with that?"

"We never mention them, dear." She pulled herself forward and regarded him with very grave concern. "We *never* mention them."

"But they don't exist!" he wailed.

Edna straightened her jacket and frowned at the floor. "Whatever gave you that idea?"

The seat vibrated beneath him. The carriage rattled.

"You're joking," he said. "You're kidding me. Zombies? There's no such thing."

Edna stood slowly, rubbing her back. Stepped into the aisle and said, "Come with me. But be careful. It's dangerous."

Confused and nervous, Frederik and Pernille followed Edna along the dusty carriage, through the door at the end, and suddenly they were outside. A howling roar, a wind tunnel. A narrow step across couplings from one coach to the next. Edna hopped the gap as though it weren't there and tugged open the door on the other side. Frederik held his breath and followed, terrified of falling. The next compartment was like the first—shabby, worn, years out of date. They struggled after Edna, trying to keep their feet as the train swayed.

"I'm *sure* it's her," Pernille whispered to him. "Isn't she amazing?"

"This way, dears! Hold on tight."

They reached the end. Another door. Another roaring

gap between carriages, railroad ties flashing by just feet below. Edna hauled them across to safety and slammed the door behind them. It was like being dragged through a battlefield.

"Here," Edna murmured. She stepped aside so they could see.

They were nearer the front of the train now, inside a carriage just like the others. Except the seats were demolished. Bent and buckled and shoved against the sides. Metal handrails had been bent like paper clips. Tables were hanging broken from the walls. The chintzy drapes were ripped. The shell was intact: the walls and the roof and most of the windows. But dividing partitions of wood and glass had been flattened. There was rubble everywhere. Fist-sized lumps of rubble. Big, jagged rocks. On the floor and on what was left of the seats. And a roaring, howling wind. Because the far end of the carriage had no door. Not anymore. In fact, the far end of the carriage was just an enormous, ragged hole, and beyond it, another. In the halfhearted light of the few remaining bulbs, they could see through the gash and all the way along the next car. More wreckage. And then Frederik looked down.

His stomach clamped tight.

His breath abandoned him.

Bile rose in his throat.

In the half-light, halfway along the carriage, staring up at him from the floor, eyes and mouth opened wide in a hideous grimace, was a severed human head.

Round the Twist

The mouth twisted in a cruel snarl. The eyes were wide open, but there were no irises, no pupils—just gray, bulging eyeballs with no center, no soul. The cheeks were deathly pale. Gray hair, gray flesh. The severed head of an old, wrinkled, balding man.

Frederik was so shocked he forgot to steady himself. The train braked and sent him tumbling toward that hideous head. "No!" he yelled. "Help!" He hit the floor among stones and debris, sliding out of control. He came to a stop just a reach away. It was horrifying. The tongue drooped from its mouth. Teeth were missing, others

chipped. An awful, colorless sag to the skin and the lips. He tried to slither backward, staring straight into those unblinking eyes.

And then Edna's sturdy shoes crunched the gravel by his ear. "I see you've met Abbot Anders," she said. "First prior of the Abbey of Valgaard."

Pernille knelt beside him. Reached out with tentative fingertips.

"Don't touch it!" he hissed.

But she did. "It's cold," she said. "Terribly cold." Then she rapped it with a knuckle, right on top. It made a dull, solid sound. "And stone dead. Literally. Feel it."

"No!"

"It's stone, my little muffin. It's made of stone."

He dared to look closer. Eyebrows, eyelids, lips, teeth. Intricate, awful detail. But she was right: Stone. A horribly lifelike carving. Not a zombie. Stone.

He was overcome with relief and embarrassment. He scrambled up and tried to recover his dignity. Brushed some of the dust from his pants.

"What is it doing here?" Pernille asked Edna. "On your train?"

"Nothing," Edna said. "Nothing at all. It's been here, doing nothing, for thirty years."

"Since the disaster," Frederik realized. "The one that no one will talk about. With the train and the mayor and Rasmus the elephant keeper."

Thirty years before, the branch line had been closed by a terrible accident, and the elephant keeper was arrested for attempting to murder the mayor. Exactly what had happened that day remained a hazy mystery.

"And *that*," Frederik said, "is one of the zombies?"

"Some might call them that, dear. Rasmus Rasmussen might."

"Were there more?"

"Many more."

"Where are they now?"

"I don't know," Edna said. "The mayor had them taken away."

The train complained into the dripping damp of the Cisterns station. Pipes and tubes and taps snaked everywhere. Water dribbled down the cracked carriage windows as though it were raining.

"So Rasmus was right?" His head was full of fragments

of information, but they wouldn't fit together. "There really *were* zombies? This was what the mayor wanted to hide?"

"She wasn't mayor in those days, but yes. It's her darkest secret. That was the day she lost her marbles, you see. The day she first went round the twist."

"She went crazy?" Pernille said. "She lost her mind?"

"No, no. Not Kamilla. A clearer, colder, more calculating mind could not be found."

"But she lost her marbles, you said. Went round the twist."

"Yes, that's right." Edna led them through the wreckage to a bench intact enough to sit on. "I was just a slip of a girl when the accident happened. Dizzy. Distracted."

Frederik glanced out the window at the damp of the Cisterns. Shuddered, watching for sinister faces at the glass.

"The branch line was wonderful in those days. We called it 'the Twist.' I don't know why; it's more of a loop. But it was the place to be seen. 'Go Round the Twist,' the billboards said. It was sort of a joke, you see. And people did, from far and wide. You could get on and off wherever you wanted with the one ticket—the Garden Park, the castle, the brewery. The zoo brought the crowds in their thousands.

The porcelain factory too. Something for everyone, the kids, the grandparents."

Pernille gazed at Edna, hypnotized.

"And it wasn't only for tourists. There were hundreds of workers converging on Frederik's Hill every day. Factory laborers, brewers, municipal officers. We made a preposterous profit. Which is how the train came to be so luxurious."

Frederik blinked at the tattered drapes and shabby seats.

"Of course, it could do with some patching now. But thirty years ago, my goodness, there wasn't another train like it. The fabrics, the polish, the grain of the wood—like the classic railways of old: the Trans-Siberian, the Orient Express. My heart would thump every time I boarded, clutching my notebook, my little pencil, so proud to be part of the finest railway there was. And you may not believe it now, my dears, but I turned a head or two in my uniform, in spite of my eccentric eye."

Frederik pretended he'd never noticed any such thing.

"Strapping young men on their way to the Cisterns. Brewers, hardened from hefting barrels. Civic officials, tall and serious in suits and ties. They would wink as I checked their tickets. But I didn't take any nonsense. Nothing would come between me and my duty to the railway." She sighed. "Can it really be thirty years?" She watched the station slide away.

"And the zombies?" Frederik asked.

"The 'marbles,' she called them. Life-size medieval statues carved from solid rock. Every church and castle in the country had a few. Over the centuries, wind and rain took their toll. Finer details eroded away. There was a TV documentary about it. And a certain ambitious young woman took note. She muscled her way forward, determined to make a name for herself."

"And her name was Kamilla Kristensen?" Pernille guessed.

"Yes. At that time Secretary for Arts and Antiquities, here on Frederik's Hill. She blackmailed someone into giving her a budget. Then she arranged for all the marbles to be brought to Frederik's Hill for restoration and a grand exhibition. The porcelain factory had special equipment. And the only way to get all that rock to the porcelain factory—"

"Was the Twist," Frederik said.

"That's right. One spring morning, we waited for hours while she marshaled them, one at a time, onto the train. Filled four whole carriages. It was the first time I saw her, and right away, I didn't like her. Barking orders and waving her little clipboard around like she owned the line."

Edna's eyes clouded. She fell quiet. She was somewhere else. Somewhere long ago. "Ole the Engineer took it slow. There were no passengers. No room. I was three carriages that way." She nodded toward the front of the train. "I'll show you."

They picked their way along the inside of the train, stepping over debris. Occasional fragments were recognizable. Here a stone hand, there an ear. They braved the gale between the cars, the broken benches, and shattered fixtures, another carriage, and another, more damage.

But the final car they reached was completely different. It was like a huge cattle car, no seats, divided into two large spaces by a hinged metal gate halfway along. Dusty floorboards. Bars at narrow windows. One enormous door in the end they had come from, and another in the side wall beyond the gate.

"I was standing just here," said Edna. "And he was standing there." She looked to the gate.

"Who?" Pernille breathed.

"Rasmus. The elephant keeper. I was dawdling, hoping

he'd notice me." She shook her head sadly. "He was the only man I ever loved."

"What happened?"

"I came through the gate to this end of the car. Then he saw me, and he seemed to falter. I didn't know why. I saw him blush. *What is it?* I wondered. And then I saw, in the palm of his hand, a tiny box. The lid was open. And something was sparkling under the lights."

"A ring?" Pernille whispered.

"He was just feet away. Right there, in front of us."

"And?"

The train rumbled like a drumroll.

"Then the door behind me flew open." She whirled around as if to confront whoever had dared to break the spell.

"Who was it?"

"Kamilla."

"The mayor?"

"She was yelling, ranting, 'What the devil is that?' and Rasmus became completely flustered. Kamilla kept shouting and shrieking and pointing, 'What's that? What's that?'"

"Pointing at the ring?" Frederik asked.

"No. At the elephant."

"There was an elephant on the train?"

"A big bull elephant. Squeezed into the far end there. But Rasmus had forgotten to close the gate. Nerves, I suppose. And the elephant was marching this way behind him. It didn't like the shouting. And the closer it came, the more Kamilla shouted. And the more she shouted, the more upset it became."

"Wait," said Frederik. He thought for a moment. "Wait, wait." Another moment. "Wait, wait, wait, wait, wait. What exactly, precisely, to be specific, was an *elephant* doing *inside* a train?"

"It was Thursday, dear," said Edna as though that explained everything.

"And?"

"And then the elephant went a bit berserk."

"Did it?"

"It did."

"I see."

"Yes."

"I don't *really* see," he explained.

"But you see the result." Edna turned and opened the

giant door leading back to the other cars. The noise was deafening, but she held it open and looked along the carriages, one after another, a trail of destruction through car after car.

"The mayor's marbles," Frederik finally understood. "She lost her *marbles*!"

"Half of them, at least. Smashed to pieces by the elephant. There were heads and arms and fractured torsos all along the train. They had to shovel them into wheelbarrows. Took weeks to unload." Edna shrugged. "It was her own fault. She shouldn't have brought them on board. Not on a Thursday. Thursday was elephant day. Rasmus would take them around to Municipal Hall for special events. We had this special car constructed for them. The tourists loved the elephants, and the elephants loved a day trip. Don't bring those statues on board on a Thursday, I told Kamilla. But did she listen? No. She was all about her career and the national news."

"Did she get into terrible trouble?"

"No," Edna said bitterly. "She didn't."

"Rasmus did," Pernille remembered. "She blamed him. She said he tried to kill her."

"And he was taken away," said Edna. "Away from here. Away from me. Forever."

“But why would she lie like that?” Pernille asked. “What could she gain?”

“What could she *lose*?” Edna said. “That was the question. What might she lose if she took the blame herself?”

“Her reputation?” Frederik said.

“Yes. And reputation was *everything* to Kamilla. Young, terribly clever, attractive too. Already a star of the borough. Now she wanted national acclaim.”

“But the marbles got smashed,” said Pernille. “On her watch.”

Edna nodded, folded her arms. “And the cover-ups began. The accident was big news for a day or two, but she had the marbles taken away and hidden. She pretended the damage was minor and they’d all be repaired. But that was a lie too. There were questions for years, of course. Churches and castles that wanted their marbles back. But she held out. Never said a word. Her career recovered, she became mayor, and in the end, the whole thing was forgotten. Faded away like it never happened.”

“Covered up just like the earthquake,” Frederik realized. “She’s been hiding the truth for decades.”

“So she isn’t worried about zombies that don’t exist,” he said. “She’s worried about zombies that do!”

"Exactly. Her greatest humiliation, the secret she has buried all these years. It would destroy her if it got out."

"It would destroy her," Frederik murmured. "So, if the Dahl Dalbys tell her that we started the rumors, or if she breaks Venkatamahesh, she'll come for us."

Pernille stared at Edna, blinking too often. "Where can we hide?" She grasped Edna's hands. "Can we stay here? With you?"

Edna chuckled. "That would be lovely. We could ride around in circles forever. No one would ever know."

A brittle smile stretched from one of Pernille's ears to the other. "Do you," she asked, hesitant, "happen, perhaps, Edna, to have any *family* you haven't seen for a while? Quite a long while? Relatives? You know?"

Edna smiled and nodded sadly. "Yes, dear. I do."

Pernille's mouth fell open in a tiny O.

"No," said Frederik. "No, Pernille."

"Are you my mama?" Pernille whispered.

The rattle of the train receded. Edna and Pernille stared at one another in the half-light.

"No," Edna said gently, kindly, finally. "No, I'm not."

Pernille's face sort of folded in on itself. She let go

of Edna's fingers. "No. Of course not. Silly. How could you be?"

"I'd be honored if I were," Edna said. "You're a delightful young lady."

"I'm adopted, you see." She couldn't meet Edna's eye.

"And I never had children. I wish I did."

"Well then. On with the mystery, I suppose. Can't dillydally. Places to be. Always someone breathing down our necks, it seems. All go. Rush, rush. Barely time to catch our breath. Where next, muffin? Onward and upward?"

Edna rested a hand on Pernille's arm. "You'll find her, dear. I know you will. Be patient."

Pernille wiped the back of her hand across her face and gave a terrific sniff. "I'm fine. It's fine. No, really. Dandy. All good. What's next?"

Frederik gave Pernille a moment to recover, then he turned to Edna. "Those marbles can ruin the mayor. They're her one weakness."

"Yes, dear."

"Then we must find them before she finds us. We must show the world what she's hiding. It's the only way to clear our names."

"You'll never find the marbles. Nobody knows where they are."

"Rasmus Rasmussen knows. He said the zombies are in the pipes. He's been down in the pipes, we know he has. He must have found them!"

Edna scowled. "Don't bring Rasmus into it. You'll upset him."

"But what choice do we have?" He took Pernille's hand. The train screeched into the gloomy station deep beneath the old elephant house. "We get off here. We're going to the zoo. We need to talk to the elephant keeper."

The Elephant in the Room

"Rasmus?" Frederik called out. "Mr. Rasmussen?"

The whitewashed public hall inside the old, abandoned elephant house echoed. Very different from the last time they were here. No chairs. No crowd. No chaos. An unlocked door led outside to hazy afternoon sunlight, washing the hillside.

Children and parents dangled over railings, watching three enormous elephants amble through the dust, swaying, spraying themselves with dirt, trunks swinging, curling, uncurling. The brand-new elephant house was a short jog away, half-buried in the hill. Darkened glass

slid silently aside to let them in, and the temperature rose by twenty degrees. A heavy aroma, dry and fruity. Muted echoes. A ramp bending down to sand and sawdust, hills of it. Sunlight filtered in from a vast, domed skylight. The twitter of birds, trapped somewhere inside, unseen. Everything was misty and golden and wonderfully warm after the chill of underground.

There was a chest-high rail. On the other side was a concrete walkway and a row of pillars of varying heights to keep the animals from the public. There was only one indoors. They had met before.

"Padma!" Pernille said.

The elephant wedged her face between two pillars and reached out with her trunk. She puffed a little cloud of straw and dust into the air. Deep, black eyes in leathery skin, a chaos of wrinkles and lines. She took a step back and then forward. Her feet met the floor with absolute silence. No vibration. None of the thunder she'd made when trapped and upset.

"Where is your keeper?" Pernille asked her.

Padma gave a huff but nothing more.

And then a door clattered open across the enormous

hall. A wheelbarrow edged through, and behind it, a slab of a man. Broad-shouldered, big-bellied, hair in every direction save for the ones it ought to be. A bulbous, red nose.

"Mr. Rasmussen!" shouted Frederik. "Over here. It's us."

The elephant keeper stopped abruptly and scowled. "What do you want?" He plowed his barrow through sand and poop until he loomed alarmingly close and alarmingly large on the other side of the railing. Green overalls, blotched with dirt and dung and possibly worse. Thick, black hairs curling out of his nostrils and his ears and his moles. A waft of awful breath.

He fished in his pocket and pulled out an enormous ball of something dark brown and misshapen. He sniffed it. Examined it. Smiled. Sank his broken, yellowing teeth deep into it, and tore off a huge, gooey hunk. "Rmm bmm," he said, with his mouth full.

"What?"

"Rmm bmm!" Little chocolate sprinkles sprayed in the air, narrowly missing them both. The elephant keeper chewed for a while, eyebrows raised, a finger pointed at his mouth as though to explain. He swallowed. Licked a smear of chocolate from the front of his teeth. "Can't resist them."

Pernille glanced at the man's bulging belly. "So I see. Rum balls. That explains a lot."

"You don't like cake?"

"As a matter of fact, I love cake. I adore cake. I hanker and yearn for it constantly."

"We've got that in common then, haven't we?"

"We have," she said. "We're like family." And then a distant light seemed to dawn behind her eyes. She tilted her head and stared at Rasmus very closely indeed.

"Oh no, Pernille," said Frederik. "Not him."

"Do you remember the first time we met?" she asked Rasmus. "Did you, by any chance, recognize me?"

Rasmus squinted. "No." He placed his nose no more than an inch from Pernille's. Breathed in her face. She recoiled and covered her nose. He stared for what seemed forever, inspecting her mouth and her eyes and her hair. His eyes narrowed to little slits. "Wait a minute. Yes! Yes, I see it now."

"You do? What? What do you see?"

"Well, *smudsig bleskift*."

"What? Tell me!"

"You can't be," said Rasmus.

"I can't be what?"

"It's impossible."

"Who am I?"

"The daughter," he breathed. "Surely you're not the daughter?"

Everything fell silent. Padma the elephant pivoted slowly and stared.

"Yes," Pernille said. "I *am* the daughter. I *am*! But whose daughter am I?"

An alarm started ringing in Rasmus's pocket. "Snack time!" he announced, and took another enormous mouthful of cake. Then he tipped his barrow on end and showered the floor with hundreds of pellets. Dark green, each the size of a thumb.

He was shoved slowly aside by Padma's trunk reaching between the pillars and gathering pellets in a pile. She scooped them high and poured them into her odd, triangular mouth. She chewed slowly, staring at Frederik and Pernille with black, shining eyes.

"Where are you going?" Pernille called. "Mr. Rasmussen?"

Rasmus had slipped away between the pillars and

around the back of the elephant. He was heading over the mounds of sand and dirt, whistling out of tune.

"Come back!" Frederik added. "Mr. Rasmussen? We need to ask you something!"

The keeper glanced back at them. "I'm busy."

"Well," Pernille said, hands on hips and buzzing with excitement, "where he goes, I shall follow." She hoisted a leg and clambered over the railing. Onto the staff-only walkway. An elephant just feet away. "Coming?" she asked, and then she was through the pillars, up to her shins in dirt and sand and whatever else the elephants had left behind.

"Pernille! You can't go up there!" Frederik looked around, desperate.

She waved a dismissive hand and accelerated up the dust hill. "It's all right. I'm family."

"You're *not,*" he said through gritted teeth. "You're *really* probably not." And now he too was struggling over the railing, heart thumping. He ducked between the pillars, sank knee deep in a mound of dust, recovered, and climbed, slipping, sliding, up the slope. "Pernille!" he shouted. "Wait for me!"

And did she? No. Of course not. When did she ever?

Rasmus disappeared through a door, Pernille in pursuit. Frederik followed into a chilly concrete corridor. No light. A sudden turn. He punched through dangling plastic slats, into another colossal space. Towering concrete walls, hazy glass ceiling.

Three inhabitants: Rasmus Rasmussen, clearly annoyed. Pernille, clearly annoying him. And the largest creature Frederik had ever seen.

It was twice the size of the others—*three* times—tall and black. A clump of thick hair above the eyes. Tusks like weapons. Great, sweeping arcs of yellow ivory, one of them needle sharp, the other shorter and capped with brass. A full-grown bull elephant, tossing side to side restlessly, rumbling. Frederik couldn't exactly hear the rumbling, but he could feel it in his belly. A deep vibration. It came in waves.

The room was a concrete box. A trap. High, flat walls. Two giant steel doors in the opposite wall. The elephant turned its colossal weight in a circle and pounded the flat of its forehead into the doors. The whole space shook, the doors, the floor, the walls, the air itself. Back the bull paced, and again it advanced, unflinching. Another deafening crash. What was it *doing*? Trying to ram its way to freedom.

It lifted its trunk and bellowed, and all the hairs stood up along the back of Frederik's neck.

Pernille and Rasmus behaved as if it simply weren't there.

"Tell me!" she said to him. "Whose daughter am I? Yours? Am I yours?"

"Mine?" Rasmus screwed up his face like a large, red walnut.

A million tons of elephant swayed toward them.

"Look out!" Frederik grabbed Pernille around the waist and pulled her to the wall. Just microseconds later and the swing of a tusk would have ripped the head from her shoulders. She slapped him about the ears as though he hadn't just saved her from certain death. And then she was after Rasmus again, running to him across the dust. She tried to embrace him, kind of, but changed her mind when she got up close.

"Mr. Rasmussen!" Frederik shouted. "Can we please address—"

The elephant thundered across the space, livid and snorting. Frederik threw himself sideways and bruised his shoulder on the concrete floor. It was dusty and dirty, and bits of straw went up his nose.

"—the elephant in the room?" he wheezed.

No one was listening. Not Rasmus, not Pernille, and certainly not the elephant. Pernille fizzed about Rasmus like a firework.

"Who is my mama? Please! I need to know. It isn't Gretchen Grondal, is it? Say it isn't her."

"I shouldn't think so," Rasmus said. "She's a miserable old witch, if you ask me."

"I *am* asking you!"

"*Why* are you asking me?"

"Because," Pernille said, and her voice seemed to fracture, "because you are my…" She hesitated, swallowed. "My real papa."

"What?"

"My real papa," she said again, this time stronger, more defiant.

Rasmus Rasmussen scratched his head and belched. "No, I'm not. Where did you get that from?"

"You *said* so," she said in a kind of squeak.

"No, I didn't."

"You did."

"No." His frown softened, and he seemed to choose

his words with more care. "No, I'm sorry if I gave you that idea, kid. I don't always know what I'm saying, see? My mouth runs away with itself sometimes."

"But you said you like cake." She mouthed something else, but no sound came.

Frederik dared to leave the wall, watching the elephant very closely indeed. "Pernille? Are you all right?"

"You and Edna," she said. Her eyes brightened. They brightened a little too much. She grabbed the elephant keeper's filthy sleeve. "You lied to protect me. Both of you. A little white lie. A kindness." She opened her hands wide. "Why didn't I see it sooner? You old lovebirds. You and her."

"Me and who?" said Rasmus, gruff and uncomfortable.

"You remember! Down in the railway? That day? The ring? You had a ring. You were about to propose."

Rasmus flushed the color of beetroot. "Who told you about that?"

"Look out!" Frederik yelped, and dragged Pernille aside as the elephant thundered her way.

Rasmus ducked under the oncoming tusk by no more than a hair. He seemed barely to notice.

"What is *wrong* with that animal?" Frederik yelled.

"Sugar rush," Rasmus croaked. "Just had his snack. Makes him fidgety."

"Fidgety?" Frederik repeated, incredulous. "You call that fidgety?"

"Also, he doesn't like doors. They make him feel trapped."

Pernille clasped her hands together as though praying. "Who is my mama?"

"I don't know. I forgot. I don't remember. I don't know what you're talking about."

"You do!"

The elephant circled the room. It angled toward the doors again and pounded into the metal once more. The ground shuddered.

"I honestly don't." Rasmus's face fell. He coughed. "I'm just an old, confused zookeeper. I understand elephants. But people confuse me. Women confuse me. Don't ask me about people or women. I'm just like him." He pointed at the elephant. "A bad-tempered old loner."

He wandered in the wake of the elephant, cooing at it like it was a kitten or something equally unlikely to trample them flat.

"But you do know something else!" Frederik said,

lurching after him. "You must. We need you to. The zombies. You know about the zombies."

Rasmus Rasmussen froze, stared at Frederik, all his color draining away. "Zombies?"

"Please tell us you know where they are!"

Top Priority

A cramped office, removed from danger. A table stained with circles from coffee cups. They could still hear the thud of that huge bull elephant ramming its door. The window rattled every time.

"Tea?" Rasmus poured boiling water into a teapot and stirred it with an old stick. "Where did I put that sugar?"

"Here," said Pernille.

Three plastic bags sat side by side on a shelf. Each packed with sugar cubes.

Rasmus took a sharp breath and grabbed her arm. "No! Not that one. *This* one. On the right."

"What's the difference?"

Rasmus chuckled, a deep, throaty rumble. "This is a zoo. The sugar isn't for humans, if you know what I mean."

Pernille gave him a moody glare. "I have no idea what you mean. Frankly, it's becoming something of a pattern."

The elephant keeper sighed. "That one there, on the right, is sugar. Straight sugar. Very good sugar, as it happens. Try it." He held the bag open. They each took a lump. Frederik's sat on his tongue for a second before he noticed. And then he noticed. It was wonderful. Incredible. Unbelievable. The sweetest, most delicate, delicious sugar he had ever tasted.

"Wow," he whispered.

"Finest coarse cane sugar from Sri Lanka. Extremely expensive." Rasmus tossed the bag back onto the shelf. "We have it specially flown in."

As the wonder ebbed away, Frederik asked, "Flown in, but not for humans?"

"For the elephants. It's what they're used to, see. Reminds them of home. They'll eat that, no complaint, anytime, no matter what I inject it with."

"You inject your sugar?"

"Yep." He set three mugs of murky liquid on the table and squeezed beside Frederik. "The bag on the left is a mix of vitamins and dietary supplements. Elephants aren't meant to be this far from regular sunshine. Messes with their hormonal balance."

"And the bag in the middle?" Pernille asked, scrutinizing it.

"Sedative."

She opened her eyes extremely wide.

"Mild," said Rasmus. "Calms them down when we need to transport them. Or for medical treatment."

"But you have tranquilizer darts for that," said Frederik.

"They're for emergencies. Sugar's kinder."

Pernille tugged on a length of her hair. "Would it perhaps be prudent to label the bags?"

Rasmus laughed. "Funny you should mention that. One morning, I wasn't paying attention. Popped a couple of the vitamin cubes in my cocoa. Didn't notice till I drank it."

"What happened?"

"Terrible. Horrible. Ruins the flavor for one thing. Tastes repulsive. And then there's the vomiting. A complete rerun of breakfast in reverse."

"How dreadful."

"It was."

"But it didn't persuade you to mark which bag is which?"

Rasmus shifted shiftily. "Can't risk that. I'm not supposed to use them myself, see. Too pricey. So I hide a bag for me alongside the ones for the animals." He rested his enormous elbows on the tabletop. It creaked. "Now." He sucked his teeth, as though building up his courage. Lowered his voice. "What's this about *zombies*?" His eyes went to the window and stayed there, watching for monsters outside.

"We need to know where they are," Frederik said. "Can you tell us? The mayor's long-lost marbles. We need to find them."

Rasmus twitched.

"We're in terrible trouble, you see. Terrible danger."

"From zombies," Rasmus nodded. "Finally, someone understands."

"No, not from zombies exactly. But from the mayor. She knows we know."

Rasmus pulled himself upright and almost toppled the table. "She knows you know about the zombies?"

"The marbles. Yes. Although she doesn't know we've seen one."

"You've *seen* one?" Rasmus pressed his back against the wall. A line of sweat appeared along his brow. His eyes were wide, his nostrils dilated, and that was a thing you didn't want to be close to. "Where?"

"Down there," Frederik said. "Underground."

"You were down *there*?"

"We were down there today. They're not really zombies. They're statues."

"*No,*" Rasmus hissed. "They are so much more than that. So much *worse*. They are old. As old as *death*. I've heard them. Their voices. I have looked into their eyes, and their eyes are old and cold and soulless."

"Yes, but stone," Frederik said. "Carved from stone."

"They *whisper*. They moan. They breathe. And when they appear in all their legions, there is ruin! Destruction."

Pernille folded her arms in front of her. "Listen, Rasmus. We know they upset you, and we understand, given how badly the mayor treated you. But you're the only person alive who can tell us where they are. And finding them is the only way to prove the mayor is lying.

If we find the marbles, we save our skins. If not, we've had it. Get it?"

Rasmus scowled. "I get it. But I can't help you. I don't know where they are."

"You once told us they're in the pipes."

"They must be. I feel them. I hear them through the floor."

"Are you sure?"

"As sure as sugar is sugar."

Frederik eyed the confusing bags on the shelf. "So not very sure at all. This is hopeless. We'll never find them. What can we do? We have to somehow get the mayor off our backs."

"Oh," Rasmus blinked. "Why didn't you say? That's easy."

"It is?"

"She's the mayor."

"Yes?"

"And what do mayors do? They plan, they budget, they prioritize. She's a prioritizer. A ruthless prioritizer. Do you know why she's chasing you?"

"Because of the zombie rumors?"

"No. Wrong. Because the zombie rumors are her highest priority. However, should a higher priority present itself, she would immediately re-prioritize, prioritizing that higher-priority priority, and deprioritizing you. See? Simple."

"Is it?" Frederik stood, stared out the window. "What higher priority is there?"

Beyond the zoo, in the Garden Park, grassy ramparts fell away from the castle to the boating lake below. At the foot of the hill there was a van and a man with a camera. He was snapping shots of the hillside, the pathways, the lake, and the lawns. Preparing for something.

"Her midsummer festival!" Frederik realized. "That's a higher priority. Her highest of all."

"So, can we make her focus on that?" Pernille said.

"How? We don't know anything about it."

"No. Except that that witch Gretchen Grondal is the caterer."

"That's something," Rasmus said.

Frederik stared at his hands. "There's less than two weeks till the festival. If we could somehow disrupt the catering preparations, it would become the mayor's top priority for sure. But how?" And his gaze strayed across the cramped, little room, up the wall, to the shelf. And three bags of sugar cubes, side by side. He stood. Reached for a bag. "Vomiting, you said?"

"Hours of it," said Rasmus. "Horrible."

"Any lasting damage?"

"Nope. Vitamins and minerals. Harmless, apart from the upset stomach."

"That's how," said Frederik. And he pocketed the bag of finest Sri Lankan coarse cane sugar on his way to the door.

They hurried through the park, snaking among the thickets and canals. Resolved, at first. Determined. But the further they got from the zoo, the more Frederik began to worry.

"This is nuts," he said. "Can we really interfere with the festival? Can we possibly get away with it?"

"I don't know, muffin. But what alternative is there?"

Approaching the northernmost gate, they passed the door in the floor. A seemingly everyday, commonplace wooden front door lay flat in the cinder path beside the murky canal. They knew what was under there: the secret pipes and tunnels that snaked beneath Frederik's Hill.

They'd been down there once. Frederik shuddered at the memory, and as they hit the street by Municipal Hall, he lost his nerve entirely. He grabbed Pernille and steered her to the Ramasubramanian Superstore. "Let's think about it," he said. "Let's hide in here. I left it unlocked this morning."

They tiptoed inside the silent store. The lights were off.

Wait.

Had he turned the lights off? He didn't remember doing that.

"Pernille! Get out of here!" he hissed. And then a hand closed tight on his shoulder. He yelped.

Pernille's eyes grew larger than ever. "Oh!" she said. And then she grinned a quite-delighted grin. "You're here! You're free! The mayor let you go?"

"Shush," said Mr. Ramasubramanian. "Come away from the window. They must not see you are here. They want to catch whoever is responsible for the zombie ballyhoo. And that is you. They are looking for you!"

"We know," Frederik said, recovered. "I'm so sorry I dragged you into it. Thank you for hiding me."

Mr. Ramasubramanian shrugged. "As though I would give you up. You are my friend. The inventor of my celebrated chococcino beverage. Consider my store your sanctuary."

"What happened at Municipal Hall?" Pernille asked. "Was it awful?"

"They grilled me," the shopkeeper said. "Barked at me. Growled and threatened. But I did not break. I told them nothing. You were not betrayed."

Pernille gave him a hug, to his evident discomfort. "You're a wonderful man," she said. "I'm so happy to see you."

"And I you," he said. "But it is a most unhappy day. I remember little other than unfortunate, unrewarding, unhappy day after unhappy day since I came to this dismal land years ago. A land without friends, save for occasional waifs and strays like you two—no offense."

"None taken. None at all. We're all waifs and strays, aren't we? We have a great deal in common."

And then something seemed to occur to her. She squinted at Venkatamahesh. Held the back of her hand in the air and examined it. She gave a tiny gasp. "Pernille Yasemin Ramasubramanian Jensen," she murmured. "Why, I'd have more syllables than the rest of the street put together." She grabbed Venkatamahesh's hand and held it alongside her own. "Look!"

"What?"

"The same color."

"Brown?"

"Yes!"

Venkatamahesh blinked a few times. "Am I missing something?"

"Yes," Pernille gasped, like she'd been holding her breath for thirteen years. "Yes, you are!"

"You're a lot taller though," Frederik said to her. "I mean, really a *lot* taller."

"A recessive gene," she declared. "Clearly."

"Clearly what?" Venkatamahesh asked.

"My darling man. Do you remember, somewhere around thirteen years ago, having, well... How should I put it?"

"A baby," Frederik said, to shorten the inevitable agony. "Did you, your wife, or anyone else, have a baby? Unusually tall and vocal. Weird white hair."

"A baby? A wife? I do not have a wife. And I do not have a baby."

"Thought not. Pernille, are you ok?"

She gazed at the floor, breathing heavily. She twisted a strand of long, white hair into an irresolvable knot.

"Pernille?" he said more kindly.

"I am glad," Venkatamahesh said, "that I do not have a wife or baby after what I heard from this mayor. She was red in the face and spitting spittle. She said if she doesn't find out who started the zombie rumor, she will round up every person of foreign origin on Frederik's Hill and send us back where we came from. Starting with me."

Frederik choked. "She can't do that. Can she?"

"She seems confident she can do whatever pleases her."

Frederik went to the window, an icy lump in his stomach. "My parents," he said. "That would include my parents. And me. And both of you. All of us." He peered over the cereals and into the street. "We have to do something. We have to make her change her priorities." He stared past the blue house, past the yellow. The duck pond, the never-open gallery, Frederik's Sushi, Frederik's Antiques. To a row of tables by the window of the Café Grondal. Customers enjoying the sunshine and refreshments.

His hand strayed to his pocket and a package of sugar cubes.

"Today," he said. "Immediately."

Sweet Dreams

They made the hastiest of plans. They cajoled Pernille's papa from his shop, marched to the Café Grondal, and found a table. There were people chatting. Lots of them. Food and drink on every table on dainty plates on dainty doilies. Neatly folded napkins. Silverware sparkling in the sun. A new banner had been draped across the front of the café: *Official Caterer to Her Ladyship's International Midsummer Festival.*

"Not for long," Frederik murmured.

Pernille's papa stretched out his legs, and they waited. From the door, pecking and fussing like a spiteful bird,

came Miss Grondal. Checking the tables. Checking the street. Checking everything whether it needed checking or not. She saw Pernille. Her back stiffened, her arms folded in indignation.

The upholsterer gave a wave. Miss Grondal wasn't impressed. In fact, she was even less welcoming than she had been earlier. "You're back," she muttered.

Pernille cleared her throat. "Miss Grondal. I owe you an enormous apology."

Even though this had been the plan, it still caught Frederik by surprise. Pernille was quite convincing.

Gretchen Grondal simply glared at her.

"This morning, I was unforgivably rude to you," Pernille went on. "I'm sorry. I don't know what got into me. It may have been gas."

The café owner didn't blink. For more than sixty seconds. Frederik counted. It was chilling. Reptilian.

"Won't you join us for coffee?" Pernille added. "A conciliatory café au lait?"

"Yes, do," said Pernille's papa. "Bygones and bridges and all of that. You've been on your feet all day, dear lady. Let us treat you to something to pep you up."

Miss Grondal's eyes flitted to the upholsterer without any other part of her moving at all. "I suppose I could spare a few minutes," she said as though nothing would pain her more.

Pernille's papa's coffee was spectacular nonetheless. A Matterhorn of cream, reaching many inches above the rim. Miss Grondal took the seat beside him. Her arm brushed his accidentally. He cleared his throat, but he didn't say a word. Neither did Pernille. But Frederik saw her flash of jealousy, her gulp. She grabbed a cake and stopped her mouth with marzipan.

Miss Grondal had a tiny espresso in a tiny cup in the palm of her scrawny hand.

"Sugar?" Pernille asked sweetly.

Would it work? Could it? All Miss Grondal had to do was pop one in her cup, and she'd be throwing up in minutes in front of her public. For several hours. That ought to get the mayor's attention. And if it didn't, they'd try it again tomorrow and every day till it did. They had no other way.

Miss Grondal's gaze settled on Pernille like a mosquito. She glanced at the china sugar bowl at the center of the table. It was piled high above the brim with white and brown, crumbly, irregular sugar cubes. They looked extraordinarily tempting. Frederik's hand went to his pocket. The bag of sugar cubes was gone. Where was it?

Miss Grondal frowned. "This bowl has been overfilled," she said.

"Overfilled?" said Pernille innocently.

"I tell my staff to fill the bowl halfway and no more."

"You used them all?" he murmured. This was not the plan. They had a plan, and this wasn't it. The plan was one or two at most.

"I think they look lovely," Pernille said. "Have one. You deserve it." And she brought the bowl closer to Miss Grondal, waving it alluringly from side to side.

"I'll take a couple," said her papa.

"No!" Pernille snapped.

"No!" Frederik yelped.

The adults stared back, suspicious now.

"Your cholesterol," Pernille explained.

"Your waistline," Frederik added.

"There's nothing wrong with my waistline," Pernille's papa protested. "I'm as fit as a ferret."

"But you've had no exercise today," Pernille said. "Whereas Miss Grondal has been laboring since dawn. If anyone deserves a boost, it's Miss Grondal. Have one. Take one. That one there. The brown one. The white one. One of each. Or two."

"*Careful,*" Frederik hissed.

Gretchen Grondal narrowed her eyes, and they were narrow enough to begin with. She reached out with pincer fingers, held them in midair, over the bowl of too many sugar cubes.

Then she dropped her hand to her lap with an irritated huff. "I always tell them: *Don't* overfill."

"Yes, but—"

"Yes but nothing. I can't rely on my own staff. It's maddening." She studied the other tables. "And would you *believe*," she said, exceedingly vexed, "the other tables are almost out?"

"Out?"

"Out of sugar! Well, these will do the trick." She grabbed the bowl and hoisted it high, beyond Frederik's desperate lunge.

"No!" he said. "Don't give them ours!"

Miss Grondal frowned at him, lips puckered. "I'll do as I please. Boys your age shouldn't be eating sugar anyway. You've an excess of energy without it."

Frederik's head was a blur now. He couldn't think what to do. He couldn't stop her. Not without making a scene. And while he was failing to think of a way, Gretchen Grondal was digging into the sugar with silver tongs.

"Oops," Pernille said.

A young couple sat at the next table along. Good looking, nicely dressed. They were holding hands across the tablecloth, gazing into each other's eyes, giggling. Miss Grondal murmured a quiet "excuse me," and transferred a pile of sugar cubes into the bowl on the couple's table. They didn't even look up.

Frederik's throat became alarmingly dry. He took a large gulp of water and it didn't help.

Two middle-aged couples at the next table along. Four cappuccinos. Miss Grondal placed two sugar cubes on each saucer. *Plink plink. Plink plink.*

The table after that was a chaos of dirty plates and scraps of food and plastic bricks. Two toddlers throwing crusts. Two parents trying to control them and argue with one another simultaneously. A selection of sugar cubes dropped into their bowl. *Plink, plink, plink.*

Pernille was watching, wide-eyed. The beginnings of

a smile. Frederik was in a cold sweat. This wasn't the *plan*. The sugar was meant for Miss Grondal. No one else.

"What's unfolding?" the upholsterer inquired. "You're like a couple of clocks, wound up and ready to cuckoo."

"No, we're not."

He smiled slightly. "You don't fool me. Something mischievous, I'll bet. Don't get caught, will you?"

"I don't think we will," Pernille said. "I have a feeling priorities are about to change."

Two elderly women in their Sunday best were tackling enormous slices of gâteau. "Thank you!" they told Miss Grondal as their sugar arrived.

"Our finest crystal organic," Miss Grondal assured them.

The elderly ladies' eyes twinkled. "Goodness!" said one. She picked up a cube and popped it into her mouth with a wicked smile. "Come along, Mildred. If you don't grab that next one, I'll eat it myself."

Her companion placed a cube on the tip of her tongue, murmuring approval. Frederik held his breath. Waited for the retching.

Nothing happened.

All along the row of tables, customers were picking

up sugar cubes and dropping them into their drinks. Some absentmindedly, midconversation. Others deliberately, savoring the moment. None were grimacing. None vomiting. Miss Grondal carried on, almost all the tables resupplied.

"It's the wrong sugar," Frederik said, realizing. "I must have picked the wrong bag. It's sugar. Straight sugar. Harmless sugar!" He didn't know whether to be exasperated or relieved.

And then, at the very far end of the long café window, a man leapt to his feet. A belligerent man with a balding head. He was staring right at Frederik and Pernille. "Hey!" he called out.

"Oh no," said Frederik.

The man made directly for them. He reached out a hand. How had he *known*?

But at the very last moment, the man came to a halt at the table next to Frederik's and completely ignored him, ignored Pernille, ignored Pernille's papa. "Someone call a doctor," he was saying.

"Oh," said Frederik. "Uh-oh."

The nicely dressed young couple were sprawled across their tabletop, eyes closed, mouths open, still holding hands. And unconscious.

The middle-aged cappuccino couples were hurrying to help. One of the women wobbled, as though an imperceptible earthquake had passed underneath. She grabbed the edge of the table, wobbled again, and sat down rather abruptly on the sidewalk, looking confused.

"What is it, darling?" her husband asked. And then his eyes glazed, his head lolled, and over he went, on top of her, out cold.

Gretchen Grondal dropped the rest of the sugar cubes on the final table, gasping, a hand to her chest. The people at that table, blazers and dresses, snooty and solemn, picked them up, put them in their mouths, and sucked while they watched.

One of the toddlers mashed a slice of buttered bread on the other's head. He did not get in trouble for this. The bread was not whipped away by an irate parent. Because both parents were taking an afternoon snooze, their chins skyward, drool dribbling down their chins.

"It's not the regular sugar," Pernille said. "It's the sedative."

"What is *happening*?" Miss Grondal yelped. She bustled down the sidewalk, veins sticking out of her neck like elastic.

A bus trundled by, passengers gawking from the window at the well-to-do of Frederik's Hill, who were wandering dazed and slumped unconscious outside the official café of Her Ladyship's International Midsummer Festival.

Miss Grondal had turned an interesting shade of purple, fully aware that something was very wrong. Something likely to interfere with her chances of catering to the queen. She stared at her snoozing clientele, rubbing her forehead and frowning, as though trying to remember something vital.

Frederik grabbed Pernille's arm and got to his feet. "Let's get out of here."

Pernille stood slowly. "Yes," she said. "Come on, Papa. We mustn't get in the way." And she smiled. She sauntered. Frederik could tell she was greatly enjoying sauntering. She sauntered by a table or two, sauntered close to Miss Grondal. "Sweet dreams," she said, and she peeled away to cross the street.

Miss Grondal's eyebrows rocketed to the very top of her forehead. "Did you have something to do with this?"

"Of course not," said Pernille. "How could we? We've no idea what you're talking about."

"Wait." Miss Grondal stared long and hard at the collapsed and unconscious outside the café. "This is familiar," she muttered. "This rings a bell."

"I assure you it doesn't," Pernille replied. "I'm simply relieved that we are thus far unaffected by whatever sickness has befallen these poor folk. Now, if you'll excuse me, I'm off to call the health inspectors at Municipal Hall."

"No!" Miss Grondal yelped. "This wasn't my fault."

"Tell that to the mayor." Pernille smiled. "Make it a priority." And they hurried across the street, got honked at by a car and abused by high-speed cyclists, Pernille's white hair bouncing in the sunshine.

Mission Accomplished

People in fluorescent-yellow jackets were hurrying back and forth outside the café. A number of ambulances were parked at impressive diagonals, blue lights spinning. Frederik, Pernille, and her papa watched from the shadows at the back of the workshop.

"So did you?" the upholsterer asked.

"Did we what?" Pernille said.

"Have something to do with all this?"

"No," she said.

"No," said Frederik.

"Not entirely," she added. "I can confidently say this wasn't our plan."

Her papa looked down on them both from his considerable height. "I would hope not. It appears to be rather serious."

"Oh, I don't think so," she replied. "Not serious. Not really."

"Should be fine," said Frederik. "All being well. In a few hours."

"And how would you two know that?"

They shifted uneasily, nothing to say.

One of the café customers was sleeping on his side on a stretcher, sucking his thumb. A paramedic rolled him to the back of an ambulance. Pried his eyelids apart and shined a flashlight into the gap.

Three identical green vans slunk along the street in a convoy and came to a halt on the corner. A small crest on the side of each. *Borough of Frederik's Hill.* Doors opened.

"Spacemen!" said Pernille.

Sci-fi figures encased from face to foot in protective biohazard suits were trying to get out of the vans. It was most ungainly. One of them tripped. It appeared they had not had very much practice. The rear doors of the vans opened too, and now there were nine of them, loping slowly across the street as though in reduced gravity. Stout, white briefcases were gripped in their white-gloved hands.

The ambulance crews moved the sleeping customers out of their way. Plastic bags were produced from giant pockets. Cups and plates and silverware were plucked from Gretchen Grondal's tables with surgical tongs.

They inspected and photographed and swabbed and sprayed each table in turn. One of them fell over and had to be helped back up. Pernille's papa roared with delighted laughter. When the surfaces were clear, they picked up the tables themselves and manhandled them awkwardly into the vans.

There was the brief whoop of a siren. A police car slid by the window. It was followed by a long, black car. The long, black car stopped in the street, between the upholstery workshop and the café. The driver got out. He was wearing a cap. He went to the far side, opened the rear door, and stood back, heads lowered and hands folded like an undertaker at a funeral.

The people in biohazard suits stopped swabbing the chairs. The paramedics paused their paramedicing. The back of a head with long, white hair emerged from the long, black car. Long, white hair tied behind in a knot. Narrow shoulders followed, in a serious coat. Her Ladyship the Mayor of Frederik's Hill.

Pernille tensed at Frederik's side.

Across the street, everyone watched the mayor. She raised a hand in the air and made a rolling gesture, as though to say, *get on with it*. The paramedics, police, and biohazard people hurried back to their activities. The mayor stepped imperiously onto the sidewalk.

In the darkened doorway to the café, Gretchen Grondal appeared. Shaken. Sheepish. She could barely look Her Ladyship in the eye.

"This is it," Frederik whispered.

Bang, bang, bang.

The three of them jumped like startled antelope.

There was a tall silhouette at the workshop door. Hands cupped to the glass, peering in.

"Get down," hissed Frederik, pulling Pernille behind a disassembled sofa. "It's Martensen. Or Mortensen. I don't know which."

Pernille's papa stared down at them. "I trust," he said, "you're going to explain all this to me later?"

"Later, yes," Pernille promised. "But get rid of him, would you? Don't let him see us."

"Who is he?"

"He's one of the mayor's detectives."

Her papa raised his eyebrows and kept on staring down.

"It's a long story," she said. "But nothing bad."

"Not bad in any way," Frederik assured him. "Don't worry about that."

"Just get rid of him. We're not here. Never have been. Pretend we've never met."

They crouched and listened in all kinds of terror as the upholsterer's footsteps echoed across the shop, and the door was unlocked and opened.

"Good afternoon," they heard the upholsterer say.

"Mr. Jensen, is it, sir?"

"It is. You're well informed. Can I help?"

"There's been an incident, sir. Across the street."

"Oh!" the upholsterer said. "*Has* there? Then that explains the small fleet of ambulances, the array of unconscious citizens, the nine people in biohazard suits, and the mayor. I'd assumed they just stopped by for tea."

"Erm," said the detective, somewhat thrown, "no.

Well, yes. Exactly. Anyway. We're conducting premises-by-premises inquiries to identify material witnesses."

"*Are* you?" said the upholsterer with tremendous enthusiasm. "*How* fantastic."

"Are you a witness, sir?"

"A witness to what?"

"To the incident, obviously."

"*Is* it obvious though?"

"Isn't it?"

"*You* tell me."

"Erm..."

"Or call back later. Take some time to think about it, if you like."

The detective fell briefly silent. Frederik so wanted to look but didn't dare. Pernille had lowered her head to the floor-boards and was trying to peer out from underneath the sofa.

"The thing is," the detective braved again, "the proprietor of the Café Grondal, whose name is Miss Grondal—"

"*Well,* I never. *What* a coincidence."

"She tells me you were at the café, sir. This afternoon, shortly before the aforementioned incident."

"*Did* she?"

"She did, sir."

"And?"

"And…were you a witness, sir? To the aforementioned…"

"Incident?" said the upholsterer.

"Yes."

"No."

"No?"

"Yes."

"Yes no, or yes yes?" the detective stumbled.

"Which?"

"I'm a little confused, sir."

"I see that." Pernille's papa allowed himself a chuckle.

Pernille too was giggling silently to herself. She glanced up at Frederik, her eyes glistening. *I love him so much*, she mouthed.

"Let me explain," her papa went on. "I was, as you say, at the café, partaking of coffee with mountains of cream, when wouldn't you know it, people started hollering and passing out all around me. It was mayhem."

"Mayhem, sir?"

Frederik thought he could hear the scratch of a pen on paper.

"Utter. Absolute. So I grasped the hand of my daughter and the even younger lad she goes about with—can't remember his name—and I hurried them to safety, as any responsible parent would. They don't need to see that sort of thing at their age, do they?"

"No, sir. No. I understand. But did you notice any suspicious activity immediately prior to the, as you put it, hollering and passing out?"

"Not at all."

"Nothing?"

"Nope."

"Are you sure?"

"On my honor as a member of the National Institution of Furniture Repairers."

"Is there such an institution, sir?"

"Probably."

"I see. It's just, well, the mayor, sir."

"The mayor?"

"She's very worried. Concerned. Alarmed, even."

"*Is* she?"

"She is. So let's keep this under our hats, sir, shall we?"

"*Hats?*"

"Keep it quiet. Don't say anything, sir. Should anyone ask. Forget it happened."

"If you say so," the upholsterer said.

"No conversations. No idle chitchat. No phone calls. No emails. No press. In particular, no press."

"And why is that exactly?"

"There's an international festival coming soon to Frederik's Hill, sir. Hadn't you heard?"

"I'd noticed the banner," said Pernille's papa. "That one over there."

Frederik dared to raise his eyes an inch above the back of the sofa. Pernille's papa was pointing across the street to the bold letters, four feet high, stretched across the front of the café: *Official Caterer to Her Ladyship's International Midsummer Festival.*

"Shoot," said the detective, whipping his cell phone from his pocket and jamming it to his ear. "Mortensen? It's Martensen. Get that banner off the front of the café right away."

Across the street, there were hurried conversations. A pair of biohazard people removed themselves from the evidence gathering and ripped the banner hastily from the wall.

A small crowd had gathered to watch since Frederik and Pernille ducked out of sight. Some were snapping pictures with their phones. A man produced a camera with an enormous lens. Martensen peeled away from the workshop door and went running. "Thomas!" he shouted. "Thomas Dahl Dalby! Put that camera away."

Pernille raised her head, and they watched as the mayor stamped up and down out there, barking orders and wringing her hands. This was far from the calm composure she typically displayed. Two stern officials led Miss Grondal to a waiting car. One of them placed a hand on her head and pushed her into the back seat.

"Mission accomplished?" said Pernille.

"Mission accomplished," Frederik said.

The upholsterer closed and locked the door. He turned to look at them. He scratched his beard. "As amusing as you seem to find this," he said, "I do not."

"No," said Pernille.

"Sorry," said Frederik.

"Was this an accident?"

"Yes," said Pernille.

"Almost entirely," Frederik added.

"*Almost* entirely?"

"Yes."

"But not *entirely* entirely?"

"Sort of."

"I see. Well, we shall talk. At length. There will be explanations. Thorough ones." He was walking steadily toward them, between the benches and half-built chairs. "Yes?"

"Very much so," Frederik said.

"Of course," said Pernille.

"Jolly good. I hope very much I shall find this funny later. Once you've reassured me there was no deliberate ill intent."

"Not very much," Pernille assured him.

"And certainly not this much," said Frederik.

"Not exactly reassuring," Pernille's papa said. "But I suppose that's a start."

"Thank you, Papa," Pernille said. She grabbed his arm and gave him her most dazzling of smiles.

Frederik watched the upholsterer melt in less than an instant. He wrapped an arm around her shoulders and held her tight. "Don't scare me like that again, do you hear me?"

"We hear you," she said. "We hear you."

The Department of Unwanted Offspring

King Frederik's Garden Park was awash with color: deep greens, light greens, the purple and red and yellow of flowers, the black and white of the strutting herons. A glorious morning on wonderful Frederik's Hill.

"I checked the web," said Frederik. "It says the mayor is looking for a new festival caterer, following certain setbacks."

"No mention of all those unconscious people?" Pernille asked.

"No. They must have woken up, I suppose."

"And if they did, they'd never incriminate us. Why would they? Only Miss Grondal went anywhere near them. It all falls on her."

"Exactly. And she definitely lost the contract. How could she not?"

"So we're in the clear," Pernille said. "Wouldn't you think? The mayor's attention is absolutely fixed on keeping Miss Grondal's mishap out of the news. All thanks to your brilliant scheme."

"Thanks to your papa too," he said. "He saved our skin when the detective came."

"He really did."

They dragged their feet through the long lawns, enjoying the sunshine, making for the canal that wove eccentrically through the park.

"Can I ask you a question?"

"Anything, muffin."

"It's delicate."

"Don't worry," she said. "I'm made of tough stuff. Papa always says so."

"Why," he asked, "when your papa is such a kind man, are you so anxious to find your birth parents?"

She didn't reply for a while. Frederik worried he'd overstepped a line. She walked a little ahead of him, to the edge of the water. "It's hard to explain," she said in the end. "But it's a very powerful urge. To know who I am. Who I really am. And what I missed."

"You might have missed something much worse."

"I know. And I'm terribly torn. I worry I'll hurt Papa. He has been such a rock for me all my life. Never let me down. But still, in the dark of night, I find myself thinking about her. Always her. My real mama. Who is she? Where is she?" She chuckled. "Of course, for a very long time, I thought she must be the mayor."

"What made you think that?"

"I was little," she said. "And very naive. But it was logical, kind of. I asked Papa how he came to adopt me. Papa said he answered an ad. It was placed by a little-known department of the borough, he told me. The Department of Unwanted Offspring. Hidden away somewhere in Municipal Hall. So I put two and two together, and came up with rather more than four. It must be the mayor, I thought. She seemed so glamorous and powerful. And her hair was just like mine. Who else could it be? But of course, I was wrong.

We know that now. Horribly wrong. I feel ashamed to have spent all that time dreaming of her when Papa was right here and doing so much to care for me."

"I'm sure he understands," Frederik said.

Pernille watched the sunlight glinting on the water, the motion of fish below the surface. Then she turned to look at him. "I still believe my real mama will come for me someday," she admitted. "I hold on to that."

Frederik nodded. Didn't know how to reply. *Yes* seemed too optimistic. *No* seemed too cruel.

"Come on." She headed over a humpback bridge and along the winding path, through trees heavy with lime-green leaves and the din of birds and the voices of children playing.

"Wait. Not that way," he said, as she veered toward the heron tree and the door in the floor and the gate to the street outside Municipal Hall.

She laughed and tossed her hair. "No need to worry about Municipal Hall anymore. We can come and go, to and fro, and wherever else we please. We're free. We're anonymous. We're off the wanted list."

"I hope so."

"We are! Of course we are."

"All right."

They wandered out by the duck pond where anyone might see them, in full view of one hundred borough offices, the lighthouse soaring skyward over their heads. And of course, she was right. No one turned a head toward them. No one called their names. No detectives came running, no alarms sounded, nothing. They were just a couple of kids out for a stroll in early summer. It felt wonderful.

"Thirsty?" Pernille asked.

"A little."

"Let's go to the workshop. See Papa. Get some lemonade."

Past the blue house and the yellow. Frederik's Antiques, Frederik's Fruit and Veg. The sun flashed and sparkled off the vast plate glass of the upholsterer's shop.

"You."

They both stopped dead. Hadn't seen her at all. Blinded by the sun in their eyes. Gretchen Grondal, blocking their way, arms folded tight.

Bicyclists bowled by, whistling, chatting on cell phones. A bus chugged in the opposite direction.

Miss Grondal stared at them, a fierce frown. "You two."

"Good afternoon," Frederik said to be polite, and he tried to pass her on her left.

She stepped quickly into his path. "You ring a bell."

"I assure you we don't," Pernille said.

"Oh yes, you do. Both of you. Especially together. You remind me of something." She gave the most awful grimace, eyes slipping upward under their lids, mouth contorted. "Why can't I remember?"

"It's nothing," Pernille said. "It's all in your mind. You must have dreamed the whole thing."

Miss Grondal's eyes popped wide open. Rolled a little. Settled back on Pernille like a laser. "Dreamed?"

"No," said Frederik.

"Let us by," said Pernille, becoming irritated now.

"That's it," she said.

"No, it isn't."

Miss Grondal's eyes narrowed to slits. "I *thought* it was a dream. I thought I had a dream. That's it. And you were in my dream. You and that boy." She went quiet, bony hands to the side of her bony face. "And Her Ladyship the Mayor. At the zoo!"

"Nonsense," said Pernille.

"I thought it was a dream." Miss Grondal stared at Pernille. Then at Frederik. Very intently. "It wasn't a dream!" she shrieked.

"You're deluded," Pernille told her.

"Deluded? I was the mayor's personally selected caterer, I'll have you know. Caterer to Her Majesty Queen Margaret!"

"Not anymore," Pernille purred. "You got what you deserve."

Miss Grondal raised a wavering finger, pointing first at Frederik and then at Pernille. "The two of you were at the zoo. And I fell unconscious for two days."

"Not at all," said Frederik, trying ever harder to get by and still failing.

"And you were at my café. And then all my customers fell unconscious. All of them. Except for you!"

"No."

"It was you!"

"Yes, it was us!" Pernille shouted from rather close. "Consider it revenge!"

Frederik choked, spluttered. "No! No, no, no!" He grabbed his head in his hands as Pernille marched away.

"Why did you say that?" he hissed. He hurried after her, buzzed by high-speed cyclists. "What have you *done*?" he wailed as he caught up to her.

"She's a horrible hag. She needed to hear it."

"No! *No!* She didn't need to hear it. She needed *not* to hear it."

"Hag," she announced, reaching the door of the upholsterer's workshop.

Frederik glanced back. Gretchen Grondal was standing, staring after them. Her little notebook and pen were out of her pocket.

"She'll tell the mayor!"

"She has no sway with the mayor anymore. We made sure of that."

"But you just undid everything we achieved! Are you out of your mind?"

Pernille turned on him, angry. "I'm disappointed in you," she said. "I make a stand and you refuse to back me?"

"It's not like that."

"Some friend you are."

She slid a key into the lock.

"I *am* your friend," he said.

She tugged the door open, stepped inside. Frederik made to follow.

"No," she said.

"What?"

She pushed the door so he couldn't get through, stared coldly at him through the glass.

"Pernille!"

"Leave me alone."

"Let me in!"

"Alone, Frederik." She closed the door, leaving him on the sidewalk. She clicked the lock, gave him a last, long, offended look, and turned away into the shadows.

She had called him Frederik. She *never* called him Frederik. He found it terribly unsettling.

As afternoon turned to evening, he sat on his bed, head in his hands. Why, oh why, had she confronted Gretchen Grondal? All she had to do was keep it zipped. Walk away. He picked at dinner, answered none of Mother's questions. He went to bed with the sun still high, almost midsummer. Stared at the ceiling. Couldn't sleep. Should have kept one of those sugar cubes. That would have knocked him out.

Drifted.

Lost track.

Wasn't sure what woke him. There were voices in the street. Perhaps that was it. The slam of a car door.

Darkness had fallen. He swung from the duvet to check the time by the clock tower like he always did. The clock tower was like a flare in the night. A secret lighthouse. A beam of light swept from side to side like a searchlight. He completely forgot to check the time. Who was up there? Who were they looking for? Him? Pernille?

No. That was ridiculous. He cleared his head with a vigorous shake.

Pernille's sat-upon house was in darkness. No sign of light or life. But across the street, there was a little of both. One window of Café Grondal was still lit, hours after closing time. There was a car in the street, headlights on. Three people stood by the car, deep in debate in the middle of the road. Two tall figures in dark clothing, and a third silhouette, a woman, thin and spiky: Gretchen Grondal.

Misgivings rolled in his gut. Could it just be someone who'd parked where they weren't supposed to? Miss Grondal was tyrannical about that. She pointed across the road, as if to say *park over there.*

Or as if pointing at the upholsterer's workshop.

"Oh no," he whispered.

He rushed to his drawer, scrabbled around under books and socks. Found his flashlight. Back to the window. He held it high and tried flashing, sending a signal. Watched Pernille's window. Nothing. Nothing at all. Tried it again. More nothing.

And then the silhouettes in the street turned his way. He closed the blind with a snap, didn't move, didn't breathe, didn't sleep for what seemed like the rest of the night.

He didn't dare knock on her door next morning. Too exposed. Walked right past. Looked for her at the station. Couldn't find her. Worried all day. After school, he hurried to their meeting places, one after another—the playground, the mall, the bicycle rack by the post office. She wasn't there. Where was she? He needed to find her.

He watched Pernille's window from his own, watching for lights to come on, golden rays slanting over the rooftops. He tried the flashlight signal again. Tried repeatedly. Nothing. Her window stayed dark.

Wednesday was the same. If only he had a cell phone. He could text her. Call her. Warn her. Apologize. Even if he didn't think he was in the wrong. But he didn't have one, and she kept hers in a tin in her closet and he'd never asked her number.

On Thursday, he went to her school. Hung around outside the gates. Asked some kids. "The weird girl?" They laughed. "We don't mix with her."

Over dinner, Father received a text. "Listen!" he said. "*All staff alert. Suspected conspiracy to derail Midsummer Festival.*"

Frederik somehow managed to swallow his mouthful.

Father's phone pinged again. "*One culprit apprehended, coconspirator sought,*" he read aloud.

"Mortimer," Mother grumbled. "No texting at the table."

Frederik placed his silverware by his plate. "Walk," he said. "Going for a walk."

"Frederik? Are you all right?"

"Fine. Fresh air. Need fresh air. Feeling queasy."

He sprinted to the upholsterer's window and peered inside. Nobody there. No one working. Closed for the day. Across the street, the café was open for the first time in days. No one seemed to be watching him. Yet. He knocked at the workshop door. No reply. He'd been too timid. He rapped on the glass. A light went on.

"Pernille?" he called. "Is that you?"

But it was Pernille's papa who appeared at the foot of the stairs and made his way between the jumble of benches. He threw the locks and bolts and peered down at Frederik from his great height.

"Is she here?" Frederik asked.

"No, she's not."

"She's not?"

"Not in."

"Is she out?"

"Gone. She is gone."

"I see." But he didn't. "When will she be back?"

The upholsterer's face twisted as if in enormous pain. "She won't be back." He was like a different man with a different voice, somewhere far away.

"What do you mean?"

"They came for her."

"Who came for her?"

"The Department of Unwanted Offspring."

Calamity

Pernille's papa retreated into the workshop, and Frederik followed. He seemed a shadow of himself. All his unruly energy was gone.

"Where did they take her?" Frederik asked.

"Back," said her papa. "They took her back. To Municipal Hall."

"I don't understand."

"Neither do I."

Overwhelming misgivings churned in Frederik's stomach. This had something to do with Gretchen Grondal

in the night. Those two tall silhouettes she directed toward Pernille's house. It had something to do with the mayor too.

"They said," Pernille's papa struggled on, "that I am not a fit father for Pernille. They said my adoption will be canceled."

"They can't do that."

"They can do whatever they choose."

The two of them stood in silence. An awful, cold silence among the untended chairs and sofas, the idle workbenches.

Something on the floor caught Frederik's eye. Underneath a workbench, among scraps of cloth. It was Pernille's pocket penlight. Abandoned. Lost. He picked it up. She took it everywhere in case of emergency. But now there was a colossal emergency, and she had dropped it. How would she signal to him?

He went back to the door and stepped onto the street. Municipal Hall and its lighthouse were just a few blocks away. Pernille was in there somewhere.

There was a sudden commotion across the way. Gretchen Grondal, emerging from her café. Two tall figures behind her. In suits. Miss Grondal was pointing. The two men stepped into the sunshine. Mortensen and Martensen. They followed Miss Grondal's outstretched finger. Stared directly at Frederik.

He bolted back inside the upholsterer's and slammed the door behind him. The whole window rattled. He ducked low and scurried into the chaos of the workshop.

"Where are you going?" asked Pernille's papa.

"I need..." He needed to get away from the window. He needed to get out of there. "I need to run. I'm sorry." And he veered through an archway and ran. Between chairs and rolls of cloth, along a tight hallway to the back door. Locked. Where was the key? There, on a window ledge. Noises behind him. Voices. Stern questions. Pernille's papa, denying knowledge. Quick, quick. Click.

He dashed outside. A narrow alley along the back, open at the end. He ran. He ran like he had never run before. He ran past his own house, couldn't go there. Too vulnerable. Along the backstreet, past the business school, down the edge of the one-time porcelain factory. He raced through the iron gates and into the Garden Park. Feet slipping on the cinder pathway, leaping over goose poop, circumnavigating pigeons. He cut behind bushes, curving away from home and the upholstery shop and the detectives, through the trees, along the mazy canal, weaving through woods and sweeping lawns.

He took every turn he came to, putting as many trees and bushes as possible between himself and his pursuers. He didn't once look back, didn't so much as glance over his shoulder. He simply sprinted. He overtook three baby carriages, two joggers, and a dog. He didn't slow till he came around a corner and realized he was heading directly toward a crowd of kids. Familiar kids. Kids he didn't want to run into: Frederik Dahl Dalby, Erica Engel, Calamity Claus. They looked up, surprised. One of them shouted something. Frederik simply ignored them. He barreled by, cut to the left, around a bush, and there, right ahead, was Municipal Hall and its lighthouse, reaching above the trees.

He couldn't go that way. He stopped dead. Looked around. Out of options. Out of breath. Forward led to Municipal Hall and certain capture. Left led out to the pond and the street, within sight of Café Grondal. To his right was the murky canal. Too wide to cross. And somewhere behind him, the detectives. He was trapped. No escape.

Unless…

Flat on the ground, by the canal, was the door in the floor.

It was an everyday kind of a door, nothing unusual

about it, apart from the fact that it lay completely flat in a public pathway and led directly underground. He had been down there once. Only a truly desperate person would ever go down there.

It looked like it was locked, latched to an iron ring in the ground. A duck was standing on it, looking at him.

There was a moment of nothing. Wind in the trees. Water slapping softly against the bank. A heron howled at him from the nesting tree.

And then he was on his knees, and the duck was flapping and squawking away to the water, and Pernille's pocket penlight was in his hand. He dug it deep between door and cinder path. He levered; he strained. He felt it give. He looked up and saw no one, but there were voices, not far away beyond the trees. He put all his strength into one almighty heave, and the padlock ripped away. The wood split. The door in the floor was no longer locked.

He got to his feet and straightened his back. He hauled the heavy door out of the dirt and flipped it over. A hole yawned beneath, completely dark. He dangled his feet over the edge, found the ladder. Climbed down into the black. A shout behind the nearest trees, a man's voice, deep, angry. Footsteps thumping on the cinder. He hauled the door over his head and down and shut and was lost in absolute darkness, damp and airless, under the ground, under the door in the floor.

His breath rasped in the silence. A strange, mournful moan rose from the pipes at the foot of the ladder.

He didn't wait. Couldn't. Slithered down the ladder in absolute darkness. There was a high-pitched noise inside his head. His feet were cold and wet. He couldn't see his feet or anything else.

The pocket penlight!

He snapped it on. Walls on every side of him. Trapped! He was trapped! No. Calm down. He'd been down here before and survived.

He shone the penlight upward. The door in the floor was ten feet above him. He stooped. The horizontal pipe led away in two directions, neither welcoming. He'd lost his bearings. Which way did he go last time he was down here? Couldn't remember.

He tried to think. And then, above him, the door in the floor groaned again. Daylight flashed round its edges. Someone was panting, hauling the door open. The detectives! They'd found him.

He skidded along the pipe, splashing, banging his head. Hands against the sides, cold, damp metal. Through the pools of water on the floor. *Splash, splash, splash*. It was stuffy. Moist and stale. The pipe curved to the right. Which way was he heading? South? North? Underneath the park? Didn't matter. He had to get away.

He tried to run. The pipe wasn't tall enough for him to stand, so he loped along like a hunchback. Came to a junction. Zigged to the left. Another junction. Zagged right. Anything to confuse his pursuers, to throw them off his tracks.

He stopped again and listened hard. No footsteps now. He waited as long as he could hold his breath. Had he lost them? Maybe.

And something bubbled up from deep inside him. Something that pushed the panic aside. Rage. A furious rage.

The mayor had taken Pernille from her papa. From her home. From the only kindness she'd ever known. It made him want to roar with anger, to thump the walls. How *could* the mayor do that? He had to help Pernille. Rescue her. How? What could he do?

He picked his way forward. The pipe rang, and water splashed. And then he heard something else. A sudden rush of dank air. A breeze against his back. What was that? A moan. A long, mournful wail. What in pity's name was that? The moan echoed and petered away. All he could hear was his own breathing.

And then footsteps. Behind him. They'd found him! Heavy breathing and the *thud, thud, thud* of feet. He ran, bashed his shoulders again and again, grazed the top of his head on unseen metal. The beam of the pocket penlight veered in every direction but no direction that helped.

"Hey!" someone called out back there in the pipes. A male voice. It rang and echoed and harried him as he hurried to escape. He took a right turn and a left—didn't have a clue where he was heading, just trying to put distance between the detectives and himself.

His foot caught against something. Maybe a rivet, maybe the lip of a section of a pipe. He went sprawling in the dark. The pocket penlight slipped from his hand. He smacked his knee, and his vision blurred, and his hands fell flat in icy water. He scrambled for the flashlight. Dropped it again. There was panting behind him. Footsteps ringing.

"Stop!" came the voice, rolling and roiling in the dark. And then, "Help!"

It echoed over and over till he was absolutely sure. The voice had cried, "Help!"

And now the footsteps were thudding really close, around the corner, any moment. He grabbed the flashlight and shone it back along the pipe into a pair of startled eyes. The full weight of a human body knocked Frederik down, into a pool of chilling water. The body tumbled over him. There was a wail and a crash and a massive splash, and the body seemed to lay still.

Then it groaned. Twisted. Curled into a ball and hugged itself in the shadows.

"I think I sprained my wrist," it said.

But it wasn't a detective's voice at all. Not the deep boom of Mortensen or Martensen. It was a boy.

Frederik pointed the penlight. A pair of eyes blinked back in the gloom. Both of them blue and one of them blackened. A puzzle of fair hair. A nose that was squashed and wonky, as though it had been broken more than once. A rather terrified expression.

"Claus?" Frederik said, astonished. "Calamity Claus? What are *you* doing down here?"

Surrounded

"What am *I* doing down here?" Calamity wailed, and it rang around the pipes. "What are *you* doing down here? I'm just following you!"

"Why? Why are you following me?"

"I don't know."

"Who's with you?"

"No one."

"No one at all? No detectives?"

"*Detectives?*" Claus almost jumped out of his pants. "*Where?*"

"All right, all right. Calm down."

"Calm down?"

"And stop repeating everything I say!" Frederik rested his back against the metal wall. He was aching in so many places they seemed to merge into one. He listened intently for more than a minute. No more footsteps. No voices. No one else was down here. Only him and, for reasons he couldn't fathom, Calamity Claus.

Calamity Claus, as everyone knew, was the most accident-prone person on Frederik's Hill. It was said that he'd been struck by lightning, a bus, a blackboard, and a number of bats, both the sporting kind and the flying rodent kind. He'd fallen off a bridge, a dock, a dog, and a bus—the same bus that struck him, coincidentally. He'd broken his tibia, fibula, ulna and scapula, fingers, nose, and toes. Most people wouldn't stand near him, for fear of getting caught up in it all.

"So," Calamity said in the dark. "What happens now?"

Another sudden rush of air whistled through the pipes with a howl and a moan.

"What was that?" he panicked.

"Nothing," Frederik told him. "Ignore it. It's normal."

"*Normal?* There's someone down here. Or some*thing*. Is there something down here?"

"Only us."

"Are you sure?"

"I'm sure." But he had to steel himself to believe that. "I'm sure," he said again.

"No zombies?"

Frederik laughed. Didn't mean to, but couldn't help it.

"It's not funny!" Calamity yelped. "Why are we down here anyway? And where's that weird girl you hang around with?"

"Something happened to her," Frederik said. "Something bad." And a darkness washed over him, crushed his spirits. Pernille was gone. Taken from her beloved papa. And from Frederik.

"I knew it," said Calamity. "I could tell you needed help."

Frederik squinted at him in the gloom. "When?"

"In the park. You ran right by us, looking scared out of your wits. I called after you. You didn't even stop."

"I was in a hurry," Frederik told him. He struggled to his feet and made sure his limbs were intact. He had a number of bruises, he was sure, and his clothes were wet and cold. "Come on. Get up. We can't stay here. Which way was I heading? That way, I think."

"How far is the exit?" Calamity asked.

"No idea."

"What?"

"You heard," Frederik sighed. The pocket penlight lit the floor a few yards ahead.

"Why are you being so unfriendly? I only wanted to help you."

"Why?"

"Because you saved me from falling off the observation tower."

"I did?"

"You did."

"I forgot about that."

"Well, I didn't," said Calamity, trudging along behind him in the damp and the dark.

Awful moans rose from the distance and rushed at them, echoing. Calamity covered his head with his arms and whimpered. "I don't like this. It's zombies."

"No, it isn't." Frederik tried to remember how he'd got out the last time he was down here. It had been luck. Fluke. He hadn't known where he was then, and he didn't know now.

Another howl from somewhere far ahead, in absolute darkness. "What was *that*?" hissed Calamity.

Frederik paused. He waited for the ghostly noise to subside. He waited a long time. To get his bearings. To make sure nothing came out of the darkness. He was cold and frightened. Not of zombies, necessarily, but of never getting out. If he never got out, who would help Pernille?

He set off again with leaden legs. His feet were freezing. His back ached from bending and his belly ached with fear. He had no idea how many turns they'd taken. No way of getting back to the door in the floor. They shuffled. They trudged. Frederik hummed to himself for a bit, but the echoes were weird and Calamity begged him to stop. They took a left and a right and another left. The pipes were corroded. Patches of rust. Strange, green stains. Little stalactites gathered under joints.

"The zombies are down here," Calamity said. "I know it."

"No, they are not."

How was he going to help Pernille? How could he get her out of Municipal Hall? The mayor had her now. The mayor was a monster.

"Help!" Calamity yelled out. "Help me! I'm trapped!" A mocking echo bounced back and forth and wouldn't stop. "Get me out!" He shoved Frederik aside and ran.

"Wait!" Frederik chased. He gave in to the fear. Ran till his lungs burned. Lost his footing, banged his knee, limped for a bit. Didn't stop. Terrible screeches rang around the pipe, taunting them.

"Help!" Calamity hollered.

The pocket penlight went out. Frederik collided with metal in absolute darkness. The penlight came on again. Flickering. The battery was going to fail. They *had* to find a way out. They sprinted. Around a corner. Wider again! The pipes were getting broader and broader. Now they could stand, and the floor was flat. A great arterial tube leading right through the hill. They didn't stop. No matter how much his legs hurt. They *had* to get out.

And there was the end! Suddenly. Dead ahead. A huge metal hatch in the end of the pipe, and a big, rusty wheel. A valve. Frederik threw himself at it. Tried to turn it. It wouldn't budge. Not even a squeak. He strained and he grunted. Calamity tried to help. Didn't. Knocked Frederik's arm, and he dropped the penlight, and they were in darkness again.

"No!" Frederik thrashed his hands around in freezing water. Where was it? Couldn't find it. Tried the valve one more time, completely blind, and suddenly it gave. Half a turn. Another.

It swung inward like a door. Dim light spilled from beyond. They ran through the gap and Frederik was suddenly falling, spinning, *thud!* Winded and still. On a chilly floor. A pain in his elbow. A twisted ankle. An urge to yell and yell and yell. But not the courage. Calamity panted and moaned at his side.

Frederik opened his eyes after a long, long wait.

It was dark, but not completely.

There were lights. Little ones, dotted here and there. Dirty brown walls, running with moisture. Tubes and ducts. Rusted joints. The empty ringing of water dripping on steel inside a vast underground chamber. The Cisterns. They had made it to the Cisterns!

"Come on," he grunted. "Follow me."

He started to crawl. His knees were soaked. He didn't have the strength to avoid the puddles. He hauled himself to an archway. Terrible howls rang around them. From every angle. Groaning. Moaning. He willed himself onward. Into a shadowy underground hall of arches and corroded metal.

"Aaaagh!" Calamity yelled. "Who's that?"

A yard ahead of them, staring at them, Frederik saw a face. A cold, gray face peering out of the shadows.

"Zombies!" Calamity howled, grabbing at Frederik's arm. "They're everywhere! We're surrounded!"

And he was right. One hundred cold, ghastly faces leered at them from the gloom.

Frederik knew right away they were statues. Of course he did. Just stone. Old, carved stone. He fought to get a grip.

After thirty seconds or so, he opened his eyes. A bit. He sort of squinted between his eyelashes.

He stayed very still. Played dead. Maybe they wouldn't see him.

No. He wasn't thinking straight. They couldn't see. They were *not* zombies. They were statues. They weren't looking at him.

And yet, they were. All of them. Hundreds of them. A yard away, a man was peering right at him from the dark. A middle-aged man from the middle ages. Eyes and mouth sunk deep in shadow. A craggy nose and the thick twists of a beard.

At his shoulder, another, deathly pale. Wrapped in

a cloak. A creepy smile. Why was it smiling like that? It wasn't. No. It was only a statue. And so was that one. Hard frown, floppy hat. Just a statue. And that one with the bulging eyes. And that one with the stick and the snarl. They were surrounded. Lost in a crowd. A lifeless crowd. Silent. Staring. Terrifying.

The mayor's long-lost marbles.

Calamity was whimpering. "Which way out of here?"

Where was the exit? There had to be an exit. They were inside a massive underground tank. Lines of lime dribbled down the rust. There was a terrible groaning coming from somewhere. In front and behind. All around them. They had to get out.

They picked their way among the marbles. It was horrible. A man in a three-cornered hat watched them. A deep crack split his chest. A woman in gray, her coat drawn close to her throat, a jagged fracture across her belly.

"I'm sorry," Calamity whimpered.

Another marble leaned toward them, one arm missing, glaring, barring the way.

"Excuse us. We'll leave."

Frederik pushed between them. He tried not to look at

them. They crowded in on him. An elderly woman, a young man in uniform, a beggar with a cup. An old man, clutching his head in anguish. Frederik swallowed a lump of fear. Told himself they were statues. Only statues.

Unnatural voices yawned from somewhere and nowhere.

"Stop that," Calamity cried out. "Please stop that."

They ran, little splashes underfoot. A dark archway broke through the wall ahead. They hurried through. The wall was many yards thick. A single candle flickered in a nook. Where candles were lit, there had to be people! Live ones. Actual ones. Warm, speaking, breathing ones you could talk to and plead for help.

They staggered into another vast chamber of damp and silhouettes. Candles in jars, burning without a flicker in the still, soggy air. More statues. Broken. Shattered. Heads scowling. Arms, hands, fingers, shoes. He shivered and shivered again. And those voices moaned in the background all the time.

Frederik followed the wall around a corner and almost shouted in relief. Stairs! Stone stairs, leading up from the wet to a black double door. A green, glowing sign. *Exit.*

He ran up the steps. He lunged at the door. Bounced

off it like a rubber ball, and was suddenly tumbling down the stairs again, knocking Calamity into a heap.

"Please, no. Please, no."

He went again, two steps at a time, placed his hands flat on the doors, and heaved with everything he had.

No movement. Not a hair. The exit was shut tight.

They huddled against the door for more than an hour. Frederik mostly kept his eyes shut. Whenever he opened them, the mayor's marbles were out there in the darkness, watching. It was terribly cold. He tried jiggling, waving his arms, breathing into his hands. It did no good.

"In case this is it," Calamity whispered in the dark, "the end for us both, I just want to say I'm sorry for the times I was mean to you. And your weird friend."

"Pernille isn't weird. Well, she is. But not the way you meant it."

The moaning in the Cisterns seemed never to stop.

"Why *were* you mean to us?" he asked.

Calamity thought for a while. "So I'd fit in. With them. Erica Engel, Frederik Dahl Dalby, Erik the Awkward. So long as they were mocking you, they weren't mocking me."

"They do it to you?"

"I have a lot of accidents. I can't help it. I get it from my dad. Anyway, I'm sorry."

"Don't worry about it."

"I do worry about it. I'm worried about everything. I'm trapped underground with hundreds of zombies. You were right all along."

The stone faces stared from the shadows. It was awful. But he *had* been right. And Rasmus had been right. The mayor's missing marbles were hidden down here, and everyone had forgotten they existed.

Or so Her Ladyship believed.

But if Frederik were to remind them, if people found out the marbles were here, the mayor would be humiliated, surely? There was a twist of anger in his belly every time he thought about the mayor. Could her secret become his weapon? A way to turn the town against her and get Pernille back?

Suddenly, something was rattling by his head. He jumped up and his leg cramped. He lost his balance and fell a few steps. Calamity fell down them all.

The doors swung open, and soft light spilled about them.

They scrambled up. Limped from the wet and cold

into a tight hallway. No one there. Stairs. A blur of daylight above. Frederik was too afraid to call out. He stumbled one painful step at a time. Up and up and into a gift shop.

He stopped, entirely surprised.

They had clambered out of a nightmare and into a gift shop?

Taking Stock

The walls of the gift shop were sloping glass. A little transparent pyramid. Outside was midevening and grass and trees. Fading postcards on racks, books on a shelf, and a layer of dust over everything. There was a desk with an ancient cash register. And a sign. *The Cisterns*, it said. *Closed to the Public. Strictly No Admittance.*

A thin man with a pale face, a clipboard, and a bunch of keys stood before them. "Who are you?" he asked. "Where did you come from?"

"No one," said Frederik. "Nowhere."

"What do you want?"

"I want to go home."

The man was wearing brown overalls. *Nordmaend Logistics*, it said on his breast. He peered down the stairs to see if anyone else was coming. "What were you two doing down there?"

"We were locked in," said Calamity.

Frederik shushed him. "What my friend means is, we were *looking* in. To something. For someone."

The man stared back. "Who?"

"The mayor."

The man's forehead creased. "Oh. Well, that's all right then. I suppose. She sent me too. I'm here to take stock. Of the items. Down there."

"Us too," said Frederik. "Taking stock. Exactly." He tried a smile.

"But that's a duplication of effort, surely?"

"True," said Frederik, nodding. "But she can't be too careful, can she?"

The man looked unimpressed. "Do you know who I am? Apparently not. Anders Andersen. Chartered stock taker, thirty-seven years. Accurate Anders, they call me. I've never miscounted in all my career."

"I see," said Frederik. "Well, we certainly can't compete with that. We should leave you to it."

The man nodded, somewhat placated. "Just out of interest, how many did you count?"

"Hundreds." Calamity shivered.

"It's hard to be exact," Frederik added. "With so many of them in pieces."

Accurate Anders groaned. "I knew there'd be a catch. There's always a catch. All right, I'd better get started, if we're going to get those marbles out of here on time."

Frederik was edging for the door, but now he stopped abruptly. "Out of here?"

"Didn't she tell you? All of them. Every one. We're shipping them out on midsummer night. While she's having that big festival in the park. Strange night to do it, if you ask me. But it's her choice. She ordered the Deluxe Expedited Service—no mess, no trace, no questions." He shrugged. "The customer is always right. If they're paying enough."

"Where are the marbles going?" Frederik asked. "Where are you taking them?"

The man chuckled. "Can't divulge," he said. "No

trace, no questions, like I said. Anyway. Better get on." And he headed down the stairs with his clipboard.

Frederik and Calamity limped outside. Evening air flooded Frederik's chest. A riot of birdsong, a dazzling sunset. They had survived. At the far side of the flat lawn that covered the underground Cisterns was the street and the curving, yellow front of King Frederik's Castle. The summit of Frederik's Hill. They were out.

But out, he realized instantly, wasn't safety. Out was exposed. Detectives were out here somewhere, hunting for him. Pernille was still in Municipal Hall, cruelly separated from her papa. What could he do? Where could he go? Who would believe he'd been trapped in the dark with those hideous marbles?

To the left of the castle, down the street, a sign stretched above bushes. *Zoo*. Rasmus would believe him. But Rasmus was out of his mind. What help would that be?

Home then. Was it safe? No way to tell, but no other option. He couldn't stay out all night.

"Claus," he said. "This has been fun."

"Fun?"

"Well, no. Not fun. You're right." He thought for

a moment. "Claus, I need a favor. I need people to know there's something in the Cisterns. And you know Frederik Dahl Dalby. And his father."

"I'll tell them," Calamity said. "I'll tell everyone. There are zombies under the hill. They'll put it in the newspaper. Everyone should be warned."

"No, wait. Not that. The mayor would come for you just like she came for me. And the media know they can't talk about zombies. It has to be something else. Something that will make them come and look without worrying about the mayor."

"Dead bodies," said Claus.

"No. That would bring the detectives."

"Money?"

"Perfect! Tell them that. Tell Frederik Dahl Dalby to tell his father there's a massive pile of money in the Cisterns. They should come quick. Before midsummer. Say it's an emergency. Say it's a lottery. First one to find it wins it all."

Calamity nodded, slightly confused.

"And, Claus, thank you for coming to help me. I'm sorry it got so weird."

And then Frederik started running toward home.

By Saturday afternoon, the chill of the Cisterns had at last left his body. He stood in the cramped back room of the Ramasubramanian Superstore, stirring a garbage can full to the brim with cold chococcino. It was backbreaking but soothing work watching the liquid slosh from side to side. Venkatamahesh was ladling it into bottles. Sheets of poorly printed labels lay on a chair. *Ramasubramanian Chococcino. Unofficial Festival Souvenir.*

"Seven days," said Frederik. "I've got seven days to reveal the marbles before the mayor gets rid of them forever. Seven days to raise the alarm and save Pernille."

"And seven days to save my business," said Venkatamahesh. "It is my pivotal moment, my toppling point. Unless I sell this chococcino, I will be ruined. We need another refrigerator."

He already had three. There were two in the back doorway and one in the tiny bathroom, buzzing loudly, every shelf loaded with bottles, ready for the festival rush, just a week away.

"I wonder if Claus delivered the message to the Dahl Dalbys?" Frederik peered beyond the apples and oranges, out the store window, across the street, to a hundred more windows, on six floors, and a lighthouse on the top. Pernille was in there somewhere. In Municipal Hall. A little-known office, hidden away. A prisoner.

"Are there dungeons?" he asked Venkatamahesh. "In Municipal Hall?" He shivered. "Did you see a door marked *Department of Unwanted Offspring*?"

"No. That sounds extremely macabre. I was taken to the mayor's office. Enormous, it was. And orderly. The crest of Frederik's Hill upon the wall, with the three little birds wearing hats. Put a little more cocoa into that batch. It looks pale."

Frederik reached for the can and levered the lid off.

"Oh no," said Venkatamahesh.

"Something wrong?"

"I think so."

"Too much cocoa now?"

"Too many detectives."

Frederik's head jerked upright. His eye went straight to the window and out to Municipal Hall. And two tall figures, picking their way through the bikes and buses.

"Quick," said Frederik. "Out the back. Run." He whipped around in a circle. "How do we open the door?"

"We cannot. It is blocked by the refrigerators."

Frederik grabbed a battered fridge. Tried to heave it aside. Bottles rattled but it didn't move. He tried the other. Tried to climb over. "We're cornered."

"Let me do the talking," said Venkatamahesh.

"They'll recognize me," Frederik yelped. "They're after me."

"You are indistinguishable from any other child."

"I'm *not*. Not to a local. My hair's the wrong color, and my accent is weird."

"You do not have an accent."

"I *do*. To them. I speak two different languages. One at home and this one everywhere else, and I can't pronounce it right."

"Only two? I spoke six as a child—Konkani, Kannada, Gondi with friends, Tamil, Hindi, English too. I agree this is a tricky tongue, but two is peanuts. You had it easy. Here." The shopkeeper grabbed a large, dirty chef's hat from a shelf and dropped it over Frederik's head. He tugged a pair of spectacles from his pocket, and Frederik put them on. Frederik couldn't see anything but blur. He developed an instant headache.

"Don't say anything in the wrong accent," said

Venkatamahesh. "Don't say anything at all. I will cover for you."

"But you'll get in trouble!"

The door of the store flew open and hit the wall. Bags of potato chips fell from a shelf. The detectives strode in, dipping their heads under the doorframe. One stood on a bag of chips and crumbs exploded across the floor. "Martensen," he growled. "And this is Mortensen. You remember us, Mr. Submarine, I'm sure."

"And what is this?" Mortensen asked, marching into the backroom.

Frederik ducked behind the garbage can.

"Contraband?" Mortensen dipped a finger in the liquid, licked it, grimaced. Spotted Frederik's hat beyond the lip. "Who's back there?"

"Chococcino!" Venkatamahesh declared. "Highest quality, lowest price."

Martensen poked his head through the doorway. "Unlicensed? Again?"

"No, no," said Venkatamahesh. He held a bottle in front of Martensen's face. "You see? It states explicitly: *unofficial* souvenir."

"Irrelevant," Martensen said. "You're under arrest. Hands behind your back."

"For making chococcino?" Venkatamahesh spluttered.

"For spreading renewed malicious rumors to discredit the Borough of Frederik's Hill."

"What rumors?" Frederik gasped.

The detective swooped to examine Frederik from no more than an inch away.

Frederik's spectacles wobbled ominously. The hat started to slip. The detective would see his foreign-looking hair and realize.

"Malicious rumors," said the detective, "of *zombies*."

"Zombies?"

"Brought to the attention of the local newspaper editor, Mr. Dahl Dalby. Today."

"Calamity," Frederik groaned. "What have you said?"

Mortensen glared at Venkatamahesh. "Is this boy involved in your conspiracy?"

"No," Venkatamahesh said. "Don't listen to the child. He has no involvement."

"Let's go, Mr. Submarine," said Martensen. "We warned you. Any more mention of zombies and there would be consequences. You're going back where you came from. Where do you come from, by the way? The Andes, was it?"

"No!" said Frederik.

"Shush," said Venkatamahesh. "I don't know who you are, child. You are clearly a very local and unremarkable person. Kindly leave my store. I need to lock up."

"But—" said Frederik.

"Be quiet," ordered Venkatamahesh. "I don't know who you are, and you have nothing to do with me or any rumors of zombies. Goodbye." And the door of the Ramamsubramanian Superstore was slamming at Frederik's back, and he was out in the street, wearing someone else's hat and spectacles, hiding his suspiciously foreign identity and the despair that welled in his eyes.

Rounded Up

He hid at home all evening, staring from his bedroom window, panicking. He said nothing to his parents. He didn't want them implicated. Everyone he knew was getting rounded up. It surely had to be illegal. Wasn't it kidnapping? Abduction? Wasn't there something about this in the Geneva Convention?

The daylight finally faded around eleven, and by four in the morning, the sky behind Municipal Hall was the yellow of dawn. He rubbed at his eyes. Hadn't slept. Couldn't sleep.

He pictured a million impossible rescues. He'd climb to the roof by the fire escape and break in through a skylight.

He'd wait till Monday morning and walk in the front door in a turban and spectacles. He'd break the windows and saw through the bars. He'd climb up from the underground railway. He'd hide inside a delivery van and ride right through the gate. He'd write to the queen. He'd write to the Geneva Convention Committee.

No, no, no.

Nothing would work.

He wondered if his friends were sleeping. Or behind one of those windows, staring helplessly back at him.

He felt powerless. He felt feeble. He felt shorter than every other kid in class. He felt like a stupid, foreign outsider who couldn't say his own name without being mocked. He felt alone.

He heard his mother calling goodbye, and watched her hurry away up the street to work. He heard his father whistling and singing as he puttered about the house. He stayed at the window for several more hours, watching the street for detectives. Eventually, he wandered down to the kitchen for lunch.

"What's up with you, young Freddy?" Father asked. "You look like you've seen a ghost. Or was it a zombie?"

He threw his arms straight out and staggered around the table, moaning.

"Stop that!" Frederik shouted. "Stop it!"

"All right," Father said, immediately worried. "All right. Just joking." He waited and watched while Frederik settled. "It's the first day of summer break. Get out and enjoy the sunshine. Find that girl you hang around with."

"You know about her?"

Father chuckled. "I'm not as old and oblivious as I look."

"She's..." Frederik faltered.

"She's what?"

"She's...gone away."

"Oh," said Father. "That's too bad."

"Yes. Yes, it is."

"Should we go to the movies? You and me?" He patted Frederik on the arm.

Frederik looked right back at that familiar face, laced with laughter lines. He so wanted to ask for help. "I can't," he said. "Not today. There's something I need to do."

"Not homework, I hope. School's over. Something fun?"

"Not really. I need to help some people."

Father raised a quizzical eyebrow.

"Father?"

"Yes, Son."

"You work for the mayor. You've worked for the mayor for a long time."

"Twelve years," Father said. "Since your mother and I first came to the country."

"Do you…respect her? The mayor?"

There was a very long pause. Father tried to mask it by munching on toast. "Well," he said eventually. "The office of mayor is very important."

"That's not what I asked. Do you respect *her*. Mayor Kristensen. Do you like her? Do you think she's a good mayor?"

"Why do you ask?" Father was avoiding the question.

"Just things that have happened. The earthquake that couldn't have been an earthquake. And now the zombies that can't possibly be zombies. And all the stuff in the news that suddenly *isn't* in the news anymore. It's all to do with the mayor, don't you think? All these secrets?"

"*Frederik,*" Father hissed.

"I just wonder what people would say if they knew—"

"Don't!" Father snapped. "You mustn't! Don't wonder. Don't ask. Don't talk about it."

They stared at one another for a long time. Not speaking. Not eating.

"It isn't safe," said Father. "Freddy. Promise me, please. Stay out of all that. It really isn't safe. Not for kids. Not for anyone."

A sudden rattle and thud made them both jump, and Mother's footsteps were on the stairs. "Yoo-hoo! I'm home. Where are you? Ah! There." She whirled into the kitchen with a small stack of mail, leafing through the letters, puzzled.

"Mortimer, love," she said without looking up, "have you seen an invitation to Her Ladyship's International Midsummer Festival? You didn't put it aside?"

"No, darling," said Father. "No, I haven't seen one."

"Only," Mother went on, "the other librarians have all had theirs, you see. And we're still waiting, aren't we?" She placed the envelopes on the table and sat down. "It's invitation only. Only where's our invitation? You didn't accidentally throw it away?"

"Of course not."

"Dorthe and Gitte and Britte and Mette and Mads got their invitations weeks ago. First-class mail; big, white envelope; crest of Frederik's Hill on the front. Everyone's got one. Everyone except Mrs. Slodzik, old Mr. Afaq, and us."

"All the foreigners," said Frederik. And something else began to nag at him. What did the mayor have planned for all the foreigners, while everyone else was at the midsummer festival?

Mother twitched. "We're not foreigners. You were born here, Frederik. It's an *international* festival, for goodness' sake."

Father's cell phone buzzed. He picked it up, distracted. "Yes? Mortimer Sandwich." He closed his eyes. "Yes, I'm home. I'm here with my family." Opened them again, lips pursed. "Hello? Anyone there?" He set the phone back on the table. "They hung up."

"Who was it?" asked Mother.

"They didn't say."

"Why would they call and ask if you're home and then hang up?" asked Mother.

A cold shudder rippled up Frederik's back. "We should get out of here," he said. "Let's go out. Somewhere. Now. Quick."

"Why?" asked Mother. "I only just got home. I

thought we might do something together, since it's your first day of break."

"Exactly. Let's get on a bus. And then a train. Let's go to the beach. A long way away. Right now."

Mother tutted and chuckled. "Maybe after I've had some lunch."

"Then I really have to run," Frederik said. And he *really* had to run. Really fast. He ran downstairs. He almost made it to the front door. And then there was a series of thunderous knocks. He stood there, paralyzed. Which way? He didn't know which way to go. He sprinted down the stairs to Mother and Father's basement bedroom. He vaulted the bed and dived inside their closet. The back wall was one of the old pipes, running right under their house.

He listened, fizzing with stress, as Father opened the door and said "Hello?"

"We'd like to come in," a deep voice replied. "We have some questions." Heavy footsteps and creaking floorboards. Frederik darted to the doorway and watched the detectives follow Father up to the kitchen. As soon as they turned out of sight, he crept up to the front door, twisted the latch, and slid outside. There was a car parked in front of the house. It had too many antennae. He looked left and right. Someone was coming. A man. Carrying a camera with an enormous lens. Thomas Dahl Dalby, the newspaper editor.

Frederik ran. Straight into the bushes in the overgrown center of the courtyard. The old factory chimney soared above him. He ducked behind thick foliage and watched.

The front door opened again. Father and Mother came down the steps looking very unhappy, Mortensen and Martensen behind them. Martensen closed the front door and ensured it was locked.

"My key," Frederik breathed. "I forgot it."

"Where is your boy?" Mortensen barked.

"Is he in trouble?" Father asked.

"He's suspected of plotting to slur the mayor's good name."

Frederik's parents were ushered into the back seat of the car with too many antennae. It roared and reversed out of the courtyard. Thomas Dahl Dalby angled his camera at the car and clicked rapidly. Frederik's mother stared, forlorn and frightened, from the back.

Frederik bolted along the winding path to the clear-ing and the hut. The crumbling brick hut at the base of the chimney was out of bounds and entirely unsafe and frequently frequented by kids he couldn't stand and who couldn't stand him. Like Calamity Claus. And what had Claus done? What had he got wrong this time? *Calamity* didn't begin to cover it. He must have mentioned the zombies. Why, oh why, had Frederik trusted him?

He scanned the apartment windows and balconies looking down on the square. No one watching. He slipped inside the hut.

"Hello? Anyone here?"

It was dark. No lamp. The pocket penlight long gone, left behind in the pipes. But for now, darkness was fine. Darkness was better than the daylight. He huddled against the back wall and watched the doorway. Heart hammering. How long could he hide here? It was out of sight, but dangerously close to home. He felt sick to his stomach. Pernille had been taken away, Venkatamahesh, and now his mother and father! It was all his fault. He had guessed the detectives were coming. Why hadn't he done more to get his parents out of the way?

"Down here, is it?"

Voices! Adults. Heading through the bushes outside.

"Got the tools?"

Tools? What tools? Stairs led down to a dark cellar beneath. Frederik ran down them. Cornered. Trapped in the shadows. His hands found the cold, metal pipe. He shuddered.

A crunch. Upstairs. Who was it?

He squeezed himself under the curve of the pipe and covered his face. Could he hide? If they didn't have a light, maybe. If they had one, he was caught.

There was a bang. A loud bang. Another. Like the bang of a hammer on a nail. And then another. And more. Someone was hammering nails up there.

A man's voice, faint. "No zombie is getting through here."

The trace of light that leaked from above seemed to dim. More banging. Dimmer still. The light was going away in the middle of the day. How could that be? Someone was up there, at the door, making the daylight go away.

And he suddenly understood.

They were boarding up the door with wood and nails.

They were sealing him inside the crumbling hut.

Supernova

When the hammering stopped and the voices melted away, Frederik climbed the stairs in darkness. Something crunched underfoot. What was that? Pieces of the old lamp they had smashed and abandoned weeks ago, when he and Pernille first scared the nasty neighbors away with their zombie story. What a trail of disaster that had caused.

A sliver of daylight squeezed between the boards across the doorway. He set his shoulder to them. Tried different angles, sweated, and grunted. He kicked with his feet, it made a din, and he continued anyway, frightened of suffocating or starving.

Then he got ahold of himself. If light was leaking through, then so was air. He wasn't going to starve for many days. And why would he go outside? Where would he go? His home was locked. He had abandoned his mother and father to the detectives.

He was better off in here, where he could do no more damage. He had no real fear of being found. The only door was blocked.

And then he remembered there was another doorway. Downstairs, in the dark cellar. An old doorway in the wall, long sealed up with bricks.

It was inky black down there. He felt for the fat, metal pipe, followed it to the wall. He traced his hands across brickwork, one pace, two paces. There. A lip. The edge of the doorway. Bricks set slightly back. He pushed. They didn't give. He chipped at the mortar between them with his fingernails. Lumps broke away and fell to the floor. He picked and scraped. There were long minutes of resistance and sudden rushes of crumbling. He couldn't see anything. He persisted, blind, till his fingers and knuckles were raw.

He needed a tool. Something jagged.

He got down on his knees and found a piece of the

lamp in the dust. A thick edge he could grip, and a point. He chipped and hacked at the mortar. The shard of glass tore it away. A brick came loose, and another, and yet another, till there was nothing left holding them up and they toppled away into nothing beyond.

Dark nothing. Cool, stale air.

"Hello?" he called, and his voice echoed differently through there. More bricks came away and now there was a trace of light. The hole grew, minute by minute, hands hurting, grit in his eyes, haunted all the while by what had happened, until eventually—it seemed like hours—the hole was big enough to dangle a leg through, feeling for the floor on the other side.

There was a sense of vast space. A haze of light, barely anything.

He clambered through and felt his way along a wall. A very long brick wall. He listened hard and heard only the thump of his heart.

He came to a door. It creaked. A wash of thin light that seemed like a glorious dawn, and steps leading up to a huge, empty room, filmed with fine, white dust. It billowed around him as he walked. He sneezed, and it spiraled in all directions. Daylight seeped through dusty windows. He was inside the disused porcelain factory. Had to be. The unconverted factory buildings. He knew them well from the outside. Enormous brick structures with ornate windows. Silent and abandoned.

He left a trail of footprints. No one had been in here for a very long time. But he'd spent his whole life playing outside. He could find his way. He had come from back there, and now he was here, with these windows up to his right. Half the factory had been converted. Apartments, the business school, the row houses where he lived. And there were two long, unconverted buildings, six floors high. He was inside one of those.

But what now? What was he going to do? What was he going to eat? Was there water? He was desperately thirsty.

He searched unlit hallways and empty rooms. Some were abandoned as though in the middle of a working day. Crockery on benches. Tools, pots, curling sheets of paper. And dust. Everywhere. Drifting around his feet as he walked, on every surface, every door handle. He found a bathroom. No water.

What was going to happen to his family? Imprisoned?

Deported? He couldn't raise the alarm. The mayor was expecting exactly that. She'd be waiting for him. He knew all her secrets, but now those secrets were no use to him. A conspiracy, she'd say. To blacken her name.

There was nothing he could do.

He found stairs, climbed a level and another. Cleared a spy hole in a grimy window, and yes, he'd been right. He could see the flats, the oak tree, the bus stop. A bus pulled up. Someone got off. Gretchen Grondal. Frederik jumped back from the window. She would see him!

But no. How could she?

He dared himself back to the spy hole, and sure enough, she was walking away. She hadn't spotted him behind the grime, two floors up in a building nobody used. Why would she even look? Ironically, in here, he was safe.

He headed upward and eastward. He wanted to see Municipal Hall. Where all his loved ones were.

He found a window overlooking the courtyard and the chimney by his house. It was a small window up in the gables, snug alongside the roof that ran the length of the row houses. At the far end was his own. Municipal Hall beyond it on the skyline. He stared for a very long time.

In the end, he decided it wasn't helping. Stepped back to explore.

In the corner of the room, set low in the wall, there was a small door half his height. He waggled the knob. There was a cloud of dust. He sneezed. And then he was looking into darkness behind the door.

He could make out some boxes. And what was that? An exercise bike?

"Someone's attic?" he whispered. He squeezed his shoulders through and crawled. Light leaked up around the edges of a hatch. What was down there? The bedroom of the first house in the row. It had to be. Mr. Hvidgaard's house. He sat for a while in silence, wondering what to do. Edged across to the far side and found a sliding panel. He levered it open, squeezed through, and into another loft. This must be Erica Engel's house. Square shapes in the gloom. Another hatch and more slivers of light. Something beside it. A flashlight? Yes! He grabbed it and flooded the attic with wonderful light. Plastic tubs of Erica Engel's hand-me-down clothes. Junk. Jars. The skeleton of a rat.

He couldn't go down into Mr. Hvidgaard's house. He'd scare the poor old man to death. And he certainly couldn't risk Erica Engel's. So he looked for another panel in the far wall, and there it was, opposite the last. This one was stiff. He had to force it, made a noise. He crossed the attics of old Mrs. Østergaard, deaf Mr. Due, cranky Mrs. Carlsen. Two houses from home, then one, and then with a final grunt, he shifted the panel that led to his own.

The flashlight splashed across familiar things. The plastic Christmas tree. The bicycle he'd outgrown. His father's records in a crate. He choked up at the sight of them.

He lifted the hatch and took a dizzying look down on his own bedroom. He took a deep breath and dropped to the bed. A cloud of porcelain dust puffed around him, hung in the air. His clothes were stiff with it. He grabbed for last night's water on the nightstand, downed it in moments, coughing.

For a long time, he lay on his back, staring up at the hatch in the ceiling, listening to the familiar ticks and creaks he had known all his life. White dust settled on the bedclothes.

Now what?

He ventured down to the living room, being very, very careful. No one was here. No detectives. No Mother or Father either.

His fingers were streaked with dried blood. His nails

were broken and scuffed. He washed his hands in a daze. Drank more water, found some food, kept the lights off, stayed away from windows. There were no notes. No phone messages.

He felt sick. Extremely scared.

He went back to his bedroom and fell asleep mideve-ning, dead tired, head aching. He woke in darkness, anxious. He stared at the attic hatch above his bed. He listened to every tiny sound. He paced the room. He tilted the slats of the blinds and peered between them, down the street.

And his head exploded.

It exploded with light. It exploded with a glare that ricocheted around inside his eyes. He clapped his hands to his face and cried out, and all he could see was the negative image of window slats seared into his eyelids. Light flooded his bedroom. It was brighter than day, brighter than the sun. He howled with the shock of it. Staggered back and toppled onto the bed. Buried his head beneath a pillow. What in the giddy name of goodness was that? He was blinded. Completely blinded.

And then darkness.

Sudden, absolute darkness.

He staggered back to the window. He pried his eyelids apart. The night slowly resolved into familiar shapes—the rooftops, the chimney pots, the same silhouettes he looked out on every night. In the distance, the clock tower above Municipal Hall. And arcing out from its topmost reaches, a beam of intense white light, sweeping in a circle above the borough, catching here a steeple, there a smokestack.

The beam of a lighthouse. A *real* lighthouse.

Sweeping away and around, picking out the brewery's huge rooftop vats, stretching over the treetops, out of sight. And then it was back! Full blaze, right in his eyes, knocking him reeling away from the window, as shocked as the first time, unable to believe how night had turned into the center of a star, an atom bomb, a supernova.

And it didn't shift. Why wouldn't it shift? It wasn't looping anymore. It was fixed directly on Frederik's window. They'd found him!

He hurled himself under the bed, and even down there, it was daybreak. Whoever was steering the searchlight had found him, the boy who started the zombie stories, the boy who sedated the café customers. He'd be rounded up like everyone else. He'd be sent to a home for unwanted offspring.

He tugged a T-shirt over his head, stuffed socks in his pockets. No time to put them on. He had to flee, had to climb. He hopped on top of the dresser, opened the hatch, clambered up inside the attic.

The light below him started to pulse. A flash. Another. Filling his bedroom with lightning, then darkness, then lightning again. He shut the hatch. He hauled the heaviest box in the attic over it, pinning it down, blocking out the supernova, sealing himself up there in the silent attics.

Every Single Rule and All at Once

He hid in the dark till long after dawn, afraid to even move. Then, he crawled through the attics to the factory. Left footprints in bewildered, swirling patterns.

He couldn't go anywhere. He was as much a prisoner as his parents. He stared from dusty windows at people passing by, kids hanging strings of little flags from lamppost to lamppost, pasting posters to walls. The mayor's festival was just five days away. She'd gain the national fame she had craved for decades. There would be no stopping her.

Frederik *had* to rescue his friends and family. Before midsummer. He had to start now.

There were only two ways to do it: bust them out, or expose the mayor as a fraud. But how? He couldn't even get out of the porcelain factory.

And then he remembered the railway.

He found a grimy escalator, out of order, deep in the bowels of the building. It plunged into darkness and a platform mired with dust. The old, blue diesel arrived in a cloud of thick exhaust. Staring surprised from a window was a familiar face beneath a familiar hat. "Porcelain Factory!" Edna said, one of her eyes on Frederik. "Next stop Frederik's Hill Central."

They sat on the faded seats and watched the shadows slide by.

"I'm going to Municipal Hall," he said.

"Second stop, dear. Why are you going there?"

"Because Pernille was arrested."

"For what?" Edna gasped.

"For knocking respectable café customers unconscious."

"She cannot *possibly* have done such a thing!"

"She didn't."

"Thank goodness."

"I did." The tunnels rattled by at top speed. "Mr. Ramasubramanian was arrested too. For nothing at all."

"But that's *terrible*. And I buy my dehydrated-noodle dinners from him. Cheapest in town. Where will I go?"

The lights of Frederik's Hill station lit the carriage end to end. There was a massive mural along the platform wall. *Frederik's Hill Welcomes the World* and a picture of the mayor, smiling, arms open.

"And my parents," said Frederik. "I have to find them. Help me find them."

"All right, dear. I will if I can."

As the train slowed again, she called out to no one. "Frederik's Hill Municipal Hall and Lighthouse." She nodded. "Here we are then. Follow me."

Another neglected platform. A door and a window in the back wall. Cracked glass, chintzy drapes that matched the ones on the train. He glimpsed a tiny room: a bed by the wall, an old oven, a table for one.

"It's modest," she said. "But it's all I can afford. Haven't had a raise in thirty years. Still, it's handy for getting to work."

She blew her whistle and the train hissed away without them. She led the way into a tunnel, lights in the ceiling, most of them blown. Another ancient wooden escalator leading way, way up. Silent and still. Very wide. Very wide indeed. It creaked as they climbed. Halfway up, Edna stopped, winded, hands on hips. They seemed to climb forever, and then they were finally at the top. A ticket hall, old machines fallen out of repair. Faded advertisements pasted to the walls. High double doors, painted red.

"Is this Municipal Hall?" he whispered.

She nodded.

Just these doors between him and his family, Pernille, and Venkatamahesh. He fell at the handle and rattled for all he was worth. Wanted to shout to them. Yell their names.

"Locked?" said Edna. "Can't say I'm surprised."

He searched the floor. Found a strip of metal. Jammed it between the doors and tried to pry them open. But the doors were like rock. The metal bent. He roared with rage and threw it at the wall.

Edna watched. "Fire doors, dear. Mahogany. Ten inches thick. You won't get through with a little twig like that."

"Then how?" Frederik howled. "There must be a way. There must be!" He banged at the door with his fist. "I have to set them free."

"And just supposing," Edna said, "that you break these

heavy fire doors down with your little tin stick. What do you plan to do next?"

"I'm going to...well, to...well..." and he trailed off, seething with frustration.

"You're going to get arrested too," she said. "And so will I. We'll run into large numbers of large policemen, just on the other side of these doors, given the noise you're making. And I'm sure they'll reunite you with your loved ones. But on the wrong side of the bars. You are more help to everyone if you're free."

Frederik rested his head against the doors. "You're right."

"Let's try to think of another way."

"There is no other way. These doors are my only way in. If I take any other route, they'll see me coming."

"Well," said Edna, "I don't see how we can remove this obstacle."

And without warning, the voice of Venkatamahesh Ramasubramanian echoed in his head.

"Remover of Obstacles," Frederik whispered. "Ganesh!"

"Bless you, dear."

"No! Ganesh. The Hindu deity. He's an elephant. Well, partly."

Edna pondered. “It’s imaginative. But I don’t know how practical.”

“It might be,” he said. “It might just be. Come on.” And he took her arm and started back toward the station. “We need to visit Rasmus.”

The train screeched into the wooden platform, deep below the elephant house. “Come up there with me.”

“No, dear, no.” She shook her head as though trying to shake something off, something she couldn’t shift. “He doesn’t remember me, I’m sure.”

“He does.”

But she wouldn’t hear it. And so Frederik climbed the twisting tunnel to the zoo alone.

He didn’t find Rasmus. Rasmus found him, standing at a narrow window, staring into the concrete cell at the massive bull elephant pounding its head into metal doors again and again, trying to bust its way through.

“He doesn’t like doors,” Frederik said.

“Hates them,” Rasmus said. “Do you need something?”

“Him. I need him.”

“The elephant?” Rasmus chuckled. “Sure. Have him back by teatime, would you?”

"Certainly," said Frederik. "Really? I can borrow him?"

Rasmus smiled. For quite a long time. Then he looked sort of confused. Then blank. Then unhappy. "No," he said. "No, no."

"No?"

"No, no, no. No, no."

"I need to knock down some doors!" Frederik whispered, checking about to make sure no one else could hear.

"No, no, no, no. Nuh-uh. Nope. Noooooo. No."

"In Municipal Hall!" Frederik hissed. "I need to get in. I need to rescue Pernille."

"The one with the hair?"

"Yes!"

"I like her."

"Yes!"

"No."

"It won't take long. I'll take him there on the train."

"The *train*? Underground? Down there? With the zombies?" Rasmus's voice got suddenly louder, his face redder. "With the *zombies*?"

"They're locked away!" Frederik told him. "And they're not zombies."

"They are zombies!" Rasmus moaned, and Frederik knew right away that he'd lost him. "Rising from the depths of the earth. Keep away from them! Keep them away from my elephants!"

"I need the elephant!" Frederik shouted.

"No!" Rasmus shouted back.

"Then what am I going to do?" he hissed through gritted teeth. "I need *help*!"

He wracked his brain for two whole days, pacing the dusty factory. He huddled at Edna's table, eating rehydrated noodles. He stared at Municipal Hall hour after hour. Nothing came. No ideas.

There was no way he was going to get an elephant. What had he been thinking? And even if he did, what then? What about the noise? How would the mayor and her staff miss colossal crashes in their basement?

The only way was to truly expose the mayor: to let the whole world know she'd been hiding those valuable marbles for thirty years to protect her own reputation. But he couldn't go to the press. And he couldn't show his face.

What would Pernille do? He laughed at the thought. Pernille would do the opposite of anything anyone expected.

She'd break the rules. *Rules are for fools*, she'd say. She'd break every single rule and all at once, if she had to.

"All right then," he murmured. "Every single rule and all at once."

He boarded Edna's train, determined now but no clearer. Time was running out. Edna came up with nothing new. The train howled into Frederik's Hill. Frederik stared, frustrated, at the people on the platform.

One of them waved.

Just a tentative how-are-you kind of wave.

"Claus?" he hissed. "Calamity Claus?"

Before Edna could stop him, he was on his feet and off the train and running across the platform, shouting, "You moron! What did you do? What did you say? They've all been taken. Pernille, Venkatamahesh, my mother and father." He grabbed Calamity's collar so hard the material ripped a little. "What did you do?" he yelled in Calamity's face.

"Sorry," said Claus.

"*You're* a wanted criminal," said Erica Engel, sliding from the shadows. "*You're* all over the news. Take your hands off our friend."

Frederik gave Calamity a push, and he tottered into Erica, knocking her backward. "Here. Have him. He's all yours."

"Wait!" Calamity said. "It was an accident."

"Don't talk to the foreigner, Claus," Erica said. "He's a stain on our borough."

Calamity's face flushed. "He isn't!" he shouted in Erica's face. Erica clearly wasn't used to that at all. "He's all right. He's not a bad kid. Once you get to know him."

"You got to know Frederik Sandwich?" she said, appalled.

"All aboard!" yelled Edna.

Frederik ran. Sprinted as fast as he could. Leapt the step and into the carriage. Turned. Was instantly knocked flat by Calamity Claus.

"Get off this train!" Frederik barked.

"I'm coming with you," Calamity said. "I'm not one of them."

"Well, you're not one of us," Frederik shouted, and then he found himself staring over Calamity's shoulder and into a pair of eyes.

"I suggest you take that back," said Edna softly.

"I won't take it back. It's all his fault. He was supposed to send the media to the Cisterns. It was simple."

"It doesn't sound very simple," Edna said.

"It wasn't," Calamity said. "I tried. I did. But it went all wrong."

"You weren't supposed to mention zombies," Frederik spat, hauling himself to his feet.

"I know. But they asked. And I got confused. And I think I might have been in shock."

Edna grabbed them both by the scruffs of their necks and tipped them onto a seat. "Hungry?" She waved a pack of suspiciously elderly cookies in their faces.

The train rattled on in the gloom. The cookies were stale but still the best thing Frederik had tasted in days. Edna watched him closely.

"We're all you've got," she told him. "A bunch of misfits, yes. But better than nothing, surely?"

He nodded, a little ashamed.

"I just want to help," Calamity said.

"Then figure out a way to show the whole of the borough where those marbles are hidden. That was your job!"

Calamity pondered, munching another cookie. He nodded and chewed, staring out the window at darkness. "Easy."

"No, it isn't. It's impossible."

"Listen!" said Edna. "Listen to him."

"Wait till Friday night," said Calamity. "Midsummer. When the marbles get moved above ground. The whole of the borough will be at the festival, just across the road."

The mayor wants them hurried away out of town. But what if that didn't happen? What if they got diverted and everyone saw them?

Frederik opened his mouth to argue. Closed it again. "Oh," he said. Claus was right. Everyone would be there. Including the mayor. And the queen. "How did you think of that?"

Calamity shrugged. "Another accident. Sometimes they're not so bad."

"Such action," said Edna, "would be very much against the rules, of course. As an employee of the borough I'm duty bound to tell you that. You can't just go around rewriting the mayor's instructions willy-nilly."

Frederik thought about that. His mouth fell open. "Yes, I can," he murmured. "Yes, I can."

The Mayor's Instructions

Frederik dropped from the attic hatch to his bed. Crept downstairs to Father's office. Municipal Hall glared over the rooftops. He closed the blinds. Had to be quick.

He flipped Father's keyboard over. There was the sticky note. Father's password: *Fr3d3r!k.* A lump appeared in his throat. He pressed a key and the monitor glowed.

Frederik's Hill Department of Rules and Regulations.

Please Enter Password.

It was so against the rules that he almost couldn't do it. But then he peeked through the slats at Municipal Hall. Father and Mother, Pernille, and Venkatamahesh locked

inside. He typed. He clicked. *Checking Credentials,* it said. And then, *Access Granted.*

He found the order he'd watched Father type a week or so back. *Mayor's Instructions Concerning Zombies.*

At the top of the page, the crest of Frederik's Hill. At the foot of the page, a reproduced signature. *Kamilla Kristensen, Mayor.*

He deleted the text in between.

Urgent, he wrote. *Mayor's Instructions. To Nordmaend Logistics, concerning my Deluxe Expedited Service.* He added more with a mix of terror and glee.

Save As.

Print.

He grabbed the sheets from the printer, snacks from the kitchen, clothes from his drawer. Found a bag and was back in the attic, panting. Rules were for fools, and he would fool them all.

One more night on the factory floor. Dawn lanced through the huge windows at four on midsummer's morning. He watched the empty streets come alive. Workers arrived in a truck and closed the roads. Rush hour was canceled. Borough holiday.

He rested. Paced. Ate some lunch. Caught the train in the afternoon when he couldn't stand to wait a moment longer.

"Where to, dear?" Edna asked, as they howled through the tunnels.

They rolled underneath Municipal Hall and its lighthouse. Frederik stared at the archway that led to the escalator that led to the door that led to Pernille and his parents.

"I need to go to the Cisterns."

"The Cisterns? The station is all locked up. No way out. Get off at the Brewery instead. Walk up the hill from there." She got to her feet. She hit the switch to open the doors. "Brewery!" she hollered. "Change here for buses to Sundby Strand." She lowered her voice. "Say hello to Torben, if you see him."

He stepped down to the platform, clutching his bag. "Who's Torben?" But his question was lost in the whistle and fumes as the train lurched away.

The platform was cracked. The walls might once have been white. Stairs led up and away. He climbed to a large, empty hall. Old beer advertisements in dusty frames. A row of doors. The first he tried swung open and away. A hallway. Voices and footsteps. A lot of them. He jumped back, alarmed. Who was out there? He reached to pull the door shut.

An enormous rubber glove closed over his wrist.

"Who's this?" A man's voice. Gruff.

Frederik was tugged through the gap and into the face of a man with not much hair. A name tag on his apron. *Noah.*

"Can you read?" the man bellowed. "What does this say?" He stabbed his finger at a sign on the door.

"*Strictly No Visitors,*" Frederik read. He gripped his bag ever tighter, terrified the man might ask what he had in there.

"Where is your party?"

Frederik glanced around. He was in a long corridor, wood panels on one side, windows on the other. Men and women in matching overalls. A rumbling somewhere. A collision of smells. Malt and bitterness and sugar. No sign of a party.

"I'm taking you to Security," said the man.

"No! Don't do that. My party is, well, I lost it."

"What did they say at the start of the tour? Do *not* lose sight of your guide. Weren't you listening?" He ushered Frederik forward. The window looked onto a cobbled courtyard. Old, industrial buildings. Tall chimneys spewing steam. He was herded through a doorway into a claustrophobic room. Enormous cylindrical tanks, peppered with fat rivets. Iron platforms overhead. Workers checking instruments. The smell was overpowering.

Up ahead, a door opened. "This way!" someone said. Well-dressed adults squeezed themselves into the room. At their lead, a woman in a shawl, a sign held over her head: *Tour Party B*. "Follow me," she called out in a singsong voice.

Frederik slipped the man's grip and was carried along by Tour Party B, through a door, and down a flight of metal steps, feet clanging.

"Boiling and sterilization," the guide called out. "Please keep to the right."

Frederik was hidden in the press of bodies. A man said something unintelligible and burst out laughing. All the tourists seemed to be foreign. Why? The festival? These must be the overseas VIPs, sightseeing before the mayor's event.

They swept along a tunnel of whitewashed stone. It was cold. Metal barrels stacked in deep dead ends. Frederik had to get out of there. But which way was out? They climbed again. Steep stairs. Huge pipes fed huge tanks. Mechanical arms stirred enormous dishes of slurry, thick liquid slurping from side to side. The air was sickly sweet.

"Mashing tuns!" the guide called out, and a dozen voices echoed in peculiar accents. "Water is drawn from the reservoir tanks up on the roof. You may have seen them." The guide waved her hand at iron pipes, disappearing into the ceiling. "Let's visit the control room!"

Frederik had no choice but to follow, up more stairs, till they were high above street level. From a window, he saw Municipal Hall in the distance. The hill in front of him, rising to the yellow walls of the castle. People *everywhere*. Thousands of them, climbing the hill and converging on the gates to the park. Parents with baby carriages, people on bicycles, toddlers towed behind in buggies. All heading for the mayor's big night. He *had* to hurry. Which way was the exit?

"These controls," the tour guide was saying, "regulate the water supply. You can read the purity on this digital display, and the hydraulic pressure here."

"And what," someone asked, "are these?"

A tangle of plumbing climbed the wall, a twisted puzzle of rusty pipes and dials. Red, rotating needles behind glass.

"That's the old water supply. The original valves and taps. No longer used."

Frederik stared. He had seen rusty valves and taps like those before. They brought back unpleasant memories. He raised his hand. He *had* to ask.

"Yes, young man?"

"Where did the old water supply come from?" He already knew the answer. He was sure of it.

The guide blinked. "That's sensitive information, actually."

"From an underground cistern at the top of Frederik's Hill," said a voice at his ear.

A portly man rested one gigantic hand on Frederik's head. He was wearing brewery overalls. He was old. A white beard and a flamboyant, white mustache. Kind, twinkling eyes. The tag on his apron said *Torben*. He pointed through the window, up the hill, toward the castle. "Up there. You can't see it. It's buried in the top of the hill. Water fed down by gravity. Massive capacity. Production in the old days was twenty times today's. But we had to stop using the Cisterns. Mayor's orders."

The tour guide hoisted her little sign and wheeled away. "Follow me, Party B. Next, the 3D Experience."

But Frederik followed Torben instead. "Excuse me, why did the mayor order that?"

Torben looked down at him, smiling. "Why do you ask?"

Frederik hesitated. "I'm just interested. In machinery, you know. And local history. Educationally speaking."

Tour Party B bustled out the doorway, leaving the two of them alone in the control room.

"And by the way, Edna says hello."

Torben's face lit up. "You're a friend of Edna's? How is she? I must say, it's nice when a youngster takes an interest in the beverage industry. Although, you won't ask too many questions about the mayor, if you've any sense."

"The Cisterns?" Frederik prompted.

"Yes. They're nearly two hundred years old. They didn't only feed the brewery. They once supplied water for the porcelain factory, the fountains in the park, houses and businesses, everything. The pipes lead in all directions, like an underground web. Some are tiny, some are huge. You could drive a bus down some of them."

"So these pipes on the wall link to the Cisterns?"

"Exactly. See that?" Torben pointed to a large lever. "That's the bypass trunk displacement unit. It connects the new supply to the old. Pull that, turn that tap, and water from our reservoir tank would shoot into the old pipes at colossal pressure." He chuckled and lowered his voice. "And these taps over here are the storage tanks. If we wanted, we could flood the Cisterns and all the underground pipes with beer." His eyes shone with amusement. "Or Volcanade."

"What's Volcanade?"

"Pop. The label says it's a hyper-effervescent antioxidant rehydration infusion with lemon, aloe, and acai. But between you and me, it's just pop. Highly-carbonated soda. Of course, the old pipes aren't in good shape. The extreme fizz would shake the town apart."

"Like the *earthquake*," Frederik murmured. He stared at Torben. "Did these taps start the vibrations in the pipes a few months back?"

Torben winced. "Don't tell anyone. The mayor went loopy when that happened. It was her own idiotic idea, of course. Testing the fountains, she said. Ridiculous. Anyway, we shouldn't talk about that. It's just we don't often get a visitor your age who's so keen." He patted Frederik's shoulder. "Stop by when you're twenty-one. We'll find a job for you."

Frederik stared from the window, toward the Cisterns, and the crowd jostling at the gates to the International Midsummer Festival. "Thank you. I'd better go."

He found his way outside in glorious sunshine. He ran across the cobbles, leaving the brewery buildings behind. Frederik's Hill was a modest rise by most nations' standards, but running up it on a warm afternoon left him breathless. At the rear of the castle, his progress slowed. Most people were inside the park now, laughing and chatting, lugging picnic hampers, eager to claim their spot on the slopes, a view of the lake and the VIP banquet. But they'd left all their bikes, trikes, buggies, and trolleys outside. The sidewalk was blocked. He stepped out into the roadway to get by.

A few stragglers, money in hand, were craning to read the menu on the side of a hot dog cart. A sour face sneered out of it. Henrik Hotdog, unloved vendor of fatty gristle and stale buns. That was strange. Why was he up here? His spot had been by the ice rink for as long as anyone remembered. A half mile away from here, at the main park entrance. "Chili dogs!" he hollered over their heads. "Low fat! Nutritious! Biodegradable!" His hot dogs were surely none of those things, but no one seemed to care.

"Frederik!" Calamity Claus peeled away from the cart with a fistful of hot dog. Almost dropped it. "Want a bite?"

"You came."

"I promised I would."

"I wasn't sure you'd make it unscathed. Let's go."

Across the street, the lawn stretched flat above the Cisterns. At its far corner, the little glass gift shop reflected the glare of the sun. Two big, white trucks were parked on the lawn beside it.

"Found you," Frederik whispered.

He rehearsed his speech. Walked to the trucks, head high. Accurate Anders appeared with his clipboard.

Frederik cleared his throat.

Accurate Anders glanced, uninterested. Sniffed. "Yes?"

Frederik fished in his bag and retrieved the printed instructions. "Urgent message! The mayor's instructions." He handed the paper to the man.

Accurate Anders studied the instructions with the precision he prided himself upon. "She wants the marbles taken to the front of the castle?"

"It's just over there." Frederik pointed. "The yellow building."

"All of the marbles?" Anders pursed his lips and made a whistling noise. "That's extremely irregular."

Frederik nodded. "But the customer is always right. If they're paying enough."

Anders went to the back of the truck and banged on the doors. They rolled up like a giant blind. A man peered out. He was dressed the same as Anders. Brown overalls. Black cap.

"Peter," said Anders. "Take a look at this."

The other man studied the order. Made the same face that Anders had made. "Don't know about that. That's a UDC."

"Exactly. Precisely." Accurate Anders turned to Frederik again. "Can't do it."

Frederik blinked back, thrown.

"Tell the mayor it's a UDC," Anders said. "Unreasonably Delayed Change. She should have read the contract. UDCs can only be accepted in the direst emergencies. Says so in the small print."

"But this *is* an emergency," Frederik stammered. "The direst emergency."

Accurate Anders gazed across the peaceful, sunlit lawns. "Doesn't seem like one to me."

Frederik's head buzzed with nothing useful. Calamity looked clueless.

"Are you all right?" Anders asked. "You look a bit shaken."

And Frederik's eyes popped all the way open. "Shaken!" he said. "Oh!" He turned on his heels and sprinted across the lawns.

He reached the brewery, red and sweating. The tour guide was closing the visitor door.

"Wait!" he shouted.

"Too late, young fellow," she told him. "Everyone is leaving for the festival."

"Forgot my jacket!" he improvised. "Something is in it. Medicine. Direst emergency!"

The woman hesitated just long enough for him to race inside.

"I know where to find it," he assured her. "Don't worry. This will only take two shakes."

Two Shakes

Ten minutes later, Frederik was climbing the hill again, gasping, flustered. Had he done it right? He wasn't sure. He'd pulled the big lever and turned a tap. Water ought to be shooting through the unstable underground pipes by now, but nothing seemed to be happening. Did he turn the correct tap? He couldn't remember. Too late to go back now.

And then he felt them.

Two shakes. Two vehement shakes. A trembling underfoot.

"Yes!" he hissed.

He ran the rest of the way, the street beginning to shudder.

The sound of an orchestra drifted from the park. The festival had started. Henrik Hotdog's line was gone. The lawn was distinctly unsteady. Frederik almost fell over.

A muscular man in brown was backing slowly out of the gift shop, struggling with the weight of a statue. He had the head. The man named Peter had the legs. Calamity Claus was helping. The tremors weren't. Accurate Anders steadied himself against the truck and made a mark on his clipboard.

Frederik ran at them. Tipped his head back and yelled as loud as he possibly could. "Earthquake! Earthquake!"

Anders stared at him. The trembling was getting stronger. Screeching birds scattered from the trees. The orchestra in the distance went distinctly off key.

"Earthquake!" Frederik hollered. "Emergency! Direst emergency!"

A fourth man in brown peered from the back of the truck. There were marbles in there already. Five of them. Sinister, leering.

"Get them to the castle," Frederik shouted. "Take the marbles to the castle."

Anders pulled a contract from his pocket and examined the small print very closely. Peter, Claus, and the other man heaved their statue onto the truck. The top of Frederik's Hill seemed to convulse. A tremor that rocked the trucks on their wheels.

Anders sighed. "All right," he said. "This seems to meet requirements after all. We'll take them to the front of the castle, per the mayor's new instructions."

"We don't have a plan for that," said Peter. "We haven't scouted the route."

"Let's do it now. Can someone lock up? We'll take these six and check for girth and ingress."

Peter took the keys and headed inside the gift shop.

"Only six marbles?" Frederik said. "The mayor wants all of them. We should take all of them."

"Six for now," said Anders. "Then we'll see."

The lawn continued to shake. The festival orchestra had given up completely. Somewhere down the hill, an emergency vehicle's siren howled. An amplified voice carried clear from the park. The mayor's voice. "Please stay calm. It's nothing, I promise!"

And then Peter stumbled out of the gift shop, a strange

look on his face. He gave a loud burp and went cross-eyed. “You won't believe this,” he said. “The Cisterns are filling up with pop!”

Heads turned. “Pop? Did you say pop?”

“Some kind of energy beverage, I'd say. A rehydration infusion. You know the type?”

“With the aloe?” Anders asked. “And the acai?”

“No, no,” said Frederik, horrified. “That's not right. It was meant to be water.”

“Definitely pop,” the man said. “I tasted it.”

“I could use some of that,” said Calamity. “This is thirsty work.” He disappeared inside the shop and down the stairs.

The wrong tap. Frederik must have turned the wrong tap. This was a disaster. Or was it really? He'd broken some rules, but that was precisely the plan. He just needed the marbles in the park, to incriminate the mayor. And some extra fizz might help.

The men climbed onto the truck and fired the engine. It curved slowly across the lawn to the street and the castle and the gates to the park. Frederik trotted behind. Would six marbles be enough? He didn't think it would be enough. He could hear anxious cries from the festival as the hill continued to shudder. The mayor made another hurried announcement, appealing for calm.

And then the truck stopped dead.

"What are you doing?" Frederik called. "Why are you stopping?"

Accurate Anders swung from the cab and disappeared around the front. Frederik hurried to see.

He found Anders at the gate that led into the top of the Garden Park.

It was an ornate iron gate. Black metal spikes with spaces in between. Six feet high, maybe ten feet wide. Accurate Anders pulled a tape measure from his pocket and verified exactly. Then he turned and measured the width of the truck. He sucked his teeth, whistled, and shook his head. "Never getting through there."

The other men dropped from the truck and stood in a group, inspecting the gate, doing nothing at all. Frederik, frantic, tugged at the gate to see if it would come off. "Perhaps if you took the fence apart?"

"Can't do that," said Anders. "That would be a UPD. Unsanctioned Property Disassembly. I'd need the mayor's signature."

"We have to get the marbles through there," Frederik fretted.

"That'll be a long job," said Peter. "We'll have to carry them one by one. Two or three men to each marble."

Frederik clambered onto the back of the truck and grabbed the first of the marbles. It had a high forehead and a cap. Its beard was long and curled. It had no eyeballs. It gave him the willies. He wrapped his arms around it, tried to move it. It wobbled, but the weight was far more than he could manage. It would fall on him and crush him.

"Fred!"

He looked up to see Calamity Claus crossing the street, moving strangely.

"Claus, you're all wet!"

"Fell in," said Calamity. "Definitely soda. Lemon. And a hint of something else." He dripped fizzing liquid all over the sidewalk. "What's the holdup?"

"The truck is too wide for the gate. And the marbles are too heavy to carry."

Calamity nodded. Pondered.. "Wheels," he said. "We need some wheels." He turned to stare along the back of the castle. "Like those over there."

"The bicycles?" Frederik said. "The tricycles?"

"The ones with the big buckets on the front. One marble in each of those. Maybe the strollers too. The baby carriages."

One of the men had overheard and wandered their direction. "That might work."

"We can still only move one at a time," Frederik said. "Unless..."

"Unless?"

Frederik ran to Henrik Hotdog's window, Calamity Claus at his heels.

"What can I get you?" Henrik said. His apron was stained, and his face was smeared with grease.

"I'm not buying."

"Not buying? No appetite?"

"We need your help."

"I don't do help," Henrik said. "Not as a rule. Although I am in a good mood. I've had a much better day than expected. When the mayor kicked me off my usual spot, I thought I was finished. I've had that place by the ice rink since my old dad's days. But it turned out there were plenty of people up here."

"The crowd inside the festival is even bigger,"

Frederik said. "Thousands of people. You should take your cart in there."

"Not allowed," Henrik grumbled. "No license."

"I can get you in."

Henrik Hotdog's greedy eyes widened. "You can?"

In no time, Henrik was wheeling his electric hot dog cart through the gate, with three heavy statues inside. The motor strained and whined with the weight. The wheels left deep grooves in the cinder path between the side of the castle and the edge of the zoo. Three stone faces stared out of the open hatch. Calamity Claus and Peter had a fourth marble in the bucket of a tricycle. One of the men had a fifth in a sturdy baby carriage. Frederik and Anders were rolling the final one along on a skateboard.

They were making progress, but it was brutal work. The marbles weren't marble at all, but maybe sandstone. They were unbelievably heavy nonetheless. The underground shudders had softened for now. Frederik could hear the mayor on the public-address system, apologizing, smoothing it over. "I hope you're enjoying our specially arranged underground massage effect." Inventing new lies. "We call it the, um, the Under Thunder. Ooh, there it goes again. How relaxing." The orchestra started up once more. There was hesitant applause. Her festival was somehow back on track.

They hauled the marbles along the side of the castle. He could finally see all the way into the park. The backs of thousands of heads spread all the way down the steep slope, to the boating lake. The crowd was enormous. Seated on the grass, on blankets, deck chairs. Dancing to the symphony composed for the event. Glasses of champagne held high, splintering the sunshine. The ground continued to shake from time to time, but incredibly, the mayor was glossing over it. The folk of Frederik's Hill believed *anything* she told them.

On a raft in the center of the lake, there was a giant stack of wood. As darkness fell, it would become the midsummer bonfire: an ancient tradition, banishing a mythical witch from the land in a blaze of defiance.

But perhaps the witch wasn't so mythical. Beyond the lake, long tables were laid with white cloths and silver settings and china plates. VIPs in dinner jackets and strapless dresses and fancy hats. A stage overlooked it all. A microphone. And the mayor. Frederik was too far away to see her expression, but she'd be schmoozing the high-powered dignitaries, ensuring nothing disrupted her long-awaited evening in the sun.

"Keep those marbles in a line," Accurate Anders called. "Make sure they're completely stable." Nothing was completely stable. Weird waves rippled through the hill. They edged along.

"Nearly there," Frederik wheezed. "Nearly there."

"*Zombieees!*"

All the men stopped and stared to their left, through the fence and into the grounds of the zoo.

Rasmus Rasmussen was thirty feet beyond, by the pelicans. Rasmus looked like a man who had seen a murder. His eyes were as wide as saucers. His mouth hung open. He was shaking, Frederik could see that from here. And he was pointing. At the marbles.

The festival orchestra swelled, drowning out Rasmus's cry. On the hillside below, no one had heard him. Yet.

"Zombies are here!" Rasmus howled.

"Be quiet!" Frederik called to him. "It's me."

"Run away! Get away!"

"Shush!"

"Help! I've got to get my elephants away from those monsters."

"No," Frederik hissed. And then a thought struck him from nowhere. An amazing, incredible thought. "Actually, yes. Yes, actually." He let go of the marble and the man alongside him staggered under its weight. "Sorry," he said. "Change of plan."

He raced to Accurate Anders. "Let's leave these marbles right here."

"Here?"

"By the fence, yes. Facing that way." He pointed into the zoo.

"Whatever the mayor wants," Anders shrugged.

"Yes. This is what she wants."

"And all the others?"

"Please bring them out of the Cisterns, every one, and arrange them along the brow of the hill. Behind the crowd. Be discreet. We don't want to distract her in the middle of her official event. She's got a terrible temper."

Frederik grabbed Calamity Claus. "Wait for me," he whispered. "Understand? Don't reveal the marbles till I get back."

"Where are you going?"

"There are some people I need to find," he said. "And this is my chance."

Back the Other Way

Frederik galloped through the zoo. The animals were indoors, despite the early-evening sunshine slanting across their enclosures. Mayor's instructions, no doubt. Nothing was to distract the public tonight. Behind him, by the castle, he could see the mayor's marbles. Six of them lined up side by side, staring through the fence.

"Rasmus! Rasmus? Where are you?"

He rushed into the muggy warmth of the new elephant house. The elephant keeper was cowering by his animals. "Zombies!" he hissed. "I warned you all. Get away! Get away!"

"Get the *elephants* away. That's the important thing, isn't it? Rasmus?"

"Yes! Get them away from the zombies."

"I know somewhere safe," Frederik said. "Let's go!"

It took a series of sprints across unsuitable terrain. Rattling keys and opening locks. Steering the females across the dust. "This way! This way!" The bull was last. He stared at Rasmus and Frederik as his steel doors swung open. Then he strode out of his cell, trumpeted at his wives and sisters and daughters, and led them up the public walkways, seeming to know exactly where to go. Sharp left, then right, to another iron door rusty with age, leading into the back of the old, abandoned elephant house.

"I can't take them down there," said Rasmus. "Not again."

Frederik pointed at the marbles.

"Aaaagh," Rasmus wailed.

And it barely mattered now anyway. Rasmus was no longer in control of the elephants. The bull was going where he wanted, and the females were following. They moved swiftly through the old elephant house and down the dark, brick tunnel to the railway. There were snuffles and snorts, cascades of dust knocked from the ceiling. Deeper and deeper into the hill. They spilled into the muted light of the station. The wooden platform groaned under their weight. Where was Edna's train?

A breeze. A wind. A rumble, thunder, a screech of metal on metal, and the blue diesel hammered into view. The elephants twisted and cowered. Rasmus tried to calm them. The bull waved his trunk from side to side, furious. Swept his tusks in a terrifying arc. Then he marched to the front of the train and the enormous loading door to the elephant car. He pulled it open with his trunk. He edged his head inside the carriage, rounded his shoulders, dipped his back, and squeezed his whole enormous frame inside the train.

"He fits," said Frederik, amazed.

"Of course he does," said Rasmus. "Elephants have traveled on trains since trains were invented."

A female followed. Then another.

"How many can get in there?" Frederik wondered.

"*What* is going on?" Edna's flushed face appeared at a door. Her hat was askew. "*Elephants?* They're banned from the railway. It isn't even Thursday!"

Rasmus turned to her. She hadn't noticed him. "We

have to get them away from here," he pleaded. "There are zombies. *Zombies*!"

Edna's hat fell to the platform. Rasmus handed it back. Edna's mouth opened, then closed, then opened again. "Rasmus," she murmured.

Rasmus watched till all the elephants had squeezed onto the train. Then he climbed up into the carriage. Frederik followed.

"Rasmus Rasmussen," he said, holding out his hand to Edna.

Her eyes had gone all vague, and her knees didn't seem to be working properly.

"And who might you be, madam?"

"You know who she is," Frederik said.

Rasmus let go of Edna's hand with a final, formal shake. "Do I?"

"Yes. You do!"

"He doesn't," Edna said with finality. "My name is Edna Brink," she told Rasmus. "Conductor on the Frederik's Hill Municipal Underground Railway."

"Charmed," Rasmus said, though somewhat distracted.

"But you've met before," Frederik said.

"We haven't," Edna told him. "No, we haven't."

"He was going to propose to you."

"No, he wasn't."

"Then who was the ring for?"

Rasmus wasn't listening at all. The elephants were filing toward them along the shattered insides of the carriages. He hurried their way to calm them.

"I don't understand," Frederik said.

"You will when you're older," Edna said, and she patted him on the shoulder. "Let's go back the other way. Counterclockwise. It's quicker." She blew her whistle—one unusually long blast followed by three short ones. The train jerked backward along the platform, heading the way it had come. "Nonstop to Municipal Hall."

"Who was the ring for?" Frederik asked.

The train rattled and swayed.

Edna looked at him. Made to speak. Opened her eyes extremely wide. Shrieked! Fizzing liquid was washing under the carriage doors and across the floor and lapping at their shoes. She crouched and sniffed. "Lemonade?" She hurried to the window. "There's lemonade up to the top of our wheels!"

"Actually," said Frederik, "it's Volcanade. With lemon, aloe, and acai."

The train slowed between dripping walls, tangled pipes. The Cisterns station was half-submerged. There was a conspicuous lemony smell.

Edna, distraught, grabbed a fire bucket and tried to scoop the soda from the floor, but the bucket filled in no time, making little impact. A wave surged along the side of the carriage. Ripples and whirlpools spiraled out. And then darkness again. The flood receded as quickly as it had come, leaving the carriage floor wet and very sticky.

"*What* is going on?" Edna called above the din.

And standing still for the first time, Frederik started to worry. What *had* he done? What had he unleashed? An earthquake, a fizzy flood, and a train full of elephants, howling through the dark. How could this end well? The brewery flashed by. Darkness again. And then soft light broke around them once more. The brakes screamed. The train stopped. The doors clattered open. Municipal Hall.

Frederik ran to the next carriage, found Rasmus with the bull. It filled the whole of the space, its wives and sisters wedged along the carriages beyond. "This is it! We get off here."

Rasmus looked at the elephant. The elephant didn't move. Rasmus shrugged. "He goes wherever he wants. You've seen him. Can't tell him anything."

"Does he?"

"He does."

"Right then." Frederik walked boldly up to the bull and his lethal tusks and his powerful trunk, head squashed against the ceiling. "We *must* rescue Pernille," he said. "My family. Please help me."

The elephant blinked.

"Pernille! You remember Pernille? I thought elephants never forget."

"Well," said Rasmus. "That's a slight misconception."

The elephant blinked again. Didn't move. Watched Frederik carefully with one big, black eye.

"And Venkatamahesh Ramasubramanian. He's here too."

The elephant lifted his head. There wasn't any space for that. Ceiling boards snapped and fell away.

Edna shrieked. "My train! Calm that animal down."

The elephant tried to turn. Couldn't.

"Here," Edna said. She hauled the heavy bucket of pop and placed it before the elephant. "Have a drink."

"Oh, that's not a good idea," said Rasmus.

But the bull dipped the end of his trunk in the bucket, inhaled, and now the bucket was empty. He curled his trunk into his mouth.

"He'll get a massive sugar rush," Rasmus said, backing away.

The elephant's eyes grew very wide indeed. He growled. He dipped his head, and then he rammed a tusk through the side of the railway carriage. He set a shoulder to the wall and spread himself to his full width and height. With a roar of ripping wood and breaking glass, the side of the carriage fell off, onto the platform.

Edna shrieked and buried her head in her hands.

"I'm sorry," Frederik told her. "I'm *really* sorry."

The bull elephant tore himself out of the train and marched along the platform. Rasmus ran after him. The females followed, one after another.

Frederik started after them. Stopped. Ran back to Edna. "Who was the ring for? Who did Rasmus want to marry, if not you?"

Edna looked up from the wreckage and sighed. "She was very attractive, that was the thing. All the young men fell for her."

"*Who?*"

"Kamilla, of course. Kamilla Kristensen."

"The *mayor*?"

"You should hurry, dear. You've got elephants wandering the corridors of power."

"Rasmus was going to propose to the *mayor*?"

"She wasn't the mayor. Not then."

"I don't know what to say." On impulse, he gave Edna a hug. She shrugged him off, startled, straightened herself, and then grabbed him again. Squeezed the breath out of him.

"I have to go!" he mumbled, face buried in the rough wool of her uniform.

"Yes. Go. Come and see me again. Bring Pernille. She's such a dear."

"I'm sorry," he said.

"You weren't to know."

"I'm sorry anyway."

"Thank you. So am I."

He sprinted along the tunnel to the steep wooden escalator. It was very wide and the ceiling was high, but the trim was splintered now, dents in the walls. Four enormous, flabby, gray behinds blocked the way. Could elephants climb? The bull was trying to. Front feet a few steps up, throwing his head around, agitated.

"Turn the escalator on!" Frederik called to Rasmus. He slapped his hand on a fat, green button, and the escalator stuttered to life, bearing the bull elephant upward. Rasmus ran after it. And now there was a procession of elephants heading up the escalator. It groaned and complained but somehow kept going. Frederik jumped aboard and rumbled all the way up to the ticket hall.

The bull was pacing the wide, dusty space, tossing his weight from side to side. The floor shook, and not from any earthquake. The bull approached the locked fire doors. Set his head against them. Growled.

"Please," Frederik said.

The bull stepped back and then forward again. He flattened those doors like they were paper. The noise was terrific. Chunks of frame and wall went flying, and the bull kept going, ramming anything in his path—walls, doors, benches, tables—Frederik running behind. Into the bowels of Municipal Hall.

A Firework

We're looking for a cell block," Frederik said. "Or dungeons. Or the Department of Unwanted Offspring."

Cleaning Supplies, said one door, *Generator*, the next. Nothing that resembled a dungeon. Narrow stairs led from the basement to glimpses of daylight somewhere above.

"The elephants won't fit up there," said Rasmus. "You're on your own."

At the top of the stairs, he found a polished lobby. Glass doors led out to Frederik's Square. There was absolute silence. No traffic outside. No voices inside. A noticeboard

listed offices. *Arts. Education. Environment. Health. Housing.* Nothing that helped.

He jogged down long, empty hallways. Peered through door after door. "Hello?" he called out, and his voice fell utterly flat. He climbed up and around to another shiny hallway. He knew what he was up against. Municipal Hall was a colossal cube, six floors high. There would be hundreds of rooms.

He tried a door. An empty office, papers on a desk. The next was the same. The next was locked. He knocked. "Is anyone there? Mother? Father? Pernille?" And not a sound. Just the thump of his own heart.

Around a corner, more doors. The first was open a little way. He gasped at the sign on the door. *Department of Rules and Regulations*. Father's office. He pushed the door open, crept inside. A vast room, half the width of the building.

No one there.

Filing cabinets, silent computers, warm evening sunshine spilling through window after window. Rows of desks. He tried to find Father's but couldn't. Maybe Father didn't have one any longer?

The windows faced toward home. He took a long look,

across the parking lot, beyond the never-open gallery, the pond, the pub, the blue house, the yellow. Somewhere over there was his bedroom window. He had stared from there to here a million times, and here he was, looking back the other way, into the gradually dipping sun.

He glanced across Frederik's Avenue. No cars, no bikes. Everyone was at the festival, or almost. A solitary woman with a dog was wandering the sidewalk. She came to the grubby window of the Ramasubramanian Superstore. She peered through the glass. Tried the door. Locked. She shrugged and wandered away.

"No! Come back!"

Who'd said that? Frederik twitched like a prairie dog, head snapping side to side. The voice had come from nearby. It was a wail of frustration in a strangely familiar accent. Frederik raced to the hallway. Tried a door. Rattled another. "Mr. Ramasubramanian?" he called, through each locked door. "Are you there? Venkatamahesh?"

"Who is that?" The voice again. Where was it coming from? This door? No. The next?

"Hello?" Frederik called. "Are you in there?"

"Are you out there?"

"Yes! Is there a key?"

"I am locked inside. With an agonizing view of the gradual, minute-by-minute ruin of the business I have striven to build over years despite the rejection of every—"

"Yes, yes. I know. Can you lever the door somehow?"

"They will hear me."

"No one will hear you. No one is here. This is our chance. Venkatamahesh? Oh!" The door was wrenched open with an ugly ripping sound. Pieces of wood scattered onto the carpet. A face appeared—a browbeaten shopkeeper holding a long piece of metal that might have been part of a drawer.

"My entrepreneurial friend!" said Mr. Ramasubramanian. "How refreshing to see you. Why are you here?"

"I'm rescuing you." He grabbed the shopkeeper's arm and hauled him into the hallway. "Are you all right?"

"No. Not at all. I have been locked in this featureless office with nothing but a photocopier, watching customer after customer come to the door of my superstore, seeking refreshments, as you predicted, on the way to the international festival. And now they are all gone, and not so much as a thimble of chococcino has been sold. My one chance has gone. I am blighted at every turn. All is lost. My store is nothing but a burden on my back. How will I ever be rid of it?"

Frederik felt extremely guilty. The chococcino had been his suggestion. But there really wasn't time for soul-searching. Only real searching. "Have you seen my parents?" he said. "Or Pernille?"

"Seen them?" said Venkatamahesh. "From the window?"

"No. Inside this building."

"I have not seen them."

"But they're here. They must be. They were arrested too, soon after you."

"Oh no. I hope they have not been deported already."

"Deported?"

"The mayor's instructions. Revealed to me during my lengthy interrogation. All interfering foreigners are to be sent back where they came from."

"But they weren't interfering! Well, Pernille was. But my parents were not."

"The mayor will not see the distinction. She is a most unpleasant woman. I myself have only seen the beige inside of that office. Twice a day they brought me food. Pickled this and pickled that and tasteless as can be."

"All right. Help me. Search this floor. Every door. Then the next floor up. I'll go higher. The fifth and sixth. They're in here somewhere and I am going to find them."

He ran around the corner. Venkatamahesh waddled. Windows faced in on the center of Municipal Hall, and to his surprise, the center of Municipal Hall was a courtyard. Rays of amber sunlight tipped in the top and lit the edge of a lawn, shrubs, six floors of windows. All these years Frederik had thought this building was a solid cube. But no. "It has a hollow heart," he said.

"Like the mayor," Venkatamahesh replied.

The clock tower struck the hour, a peel and then a clang. Another. Frederik counted. Seven in the evening already.

"We must hurry," he said. "Shout if you find her. Shout the building down!" And he was running up another flight of stairs. Where was she? Fifth floor. Another hallway, and lines of photographs. Portraits. Middle-aged men, bewhiskered and ancient. All the mayors of Frederik's Hill. 1860, Carl Christian Falck. 1870, Søren Bramming. Stiff collars and stern expressions. Mustaches shrinking through the decades, hair lengthening, women here and there. The seventies, the eighties. Terrible ties and dreadful jackets. And then a face that struck a chill into Frederik's stomach.

Edna was right. Kamilla Kristensen had been a striking young woman, with those cheekbones and those eyes and her hair so fair. And here she was again. And again, and again. Aging gracefully through the years, reelected and rephotographed every few, monopolizing the office of mayor for decades.

It took less than ten minutes to rattle the knobs and try the doors, and then he was up the wide marble stairs again. The final floor. The sixth and top. The doors were farther apart. He pushed one open and stared into an elegant corner office, golden with sunlight. An enormous, orderly desk at the center of an enormous, orderly floor, and the crest of the mayor of Frederik's Hill on the wall.

This had to be the mayor's room. He stepped inside. A window gave a sweeping view across Frederik's Square and down Frederik's Avenue. Another faced the setting sun. He could see his house. His bedroom window above the roofs. The factory chimney pointing skyward.

"I'm telling you I saw something."

Frederik jumped. A voice!

"On the security camera?" Another.

Venkatamahesh? No. Deeper. Local. He threw himself under the enormous orderly desk. Footsteps. Coming along the hallway, closer and closer.

"A *hippo*, you said?"

"Something like that." The detectives, Mortensen and Martensen.

"In Municipal Hall?" The voices paused at the door.

"Who left this door open?"

"Her Ladyship?"

"She never leaves it open. She has a closed-door policy."

Frederik stayed as still as one of the mayor's marbles under the desk.

"No hippos in here."

The door clicked shut. And then the voices were drifting away, along the hallway. He waited a minute, maybe more. Then he tiptoed to the door. Let himself out and crept along the corridor. A sudden wobble passed through the floor, the doors rattled, and voices were coming back.

"Did you feel that?"

"Yes, and I heard something too. What does a hippo sound like?"

"Similar to a tapir, I believe."

"What does a tapir sound like?"

Frederik fled down the hallway, looking for somewhere, anywhere to hide. Reached a corner. A passage with an arched door, right at the end. He ran all the way. Tried the knob. Pulled. Nothing. Locked? No. Opened the other way. He threw himself through, and where was he now? At the foot of a flight of stairs, winding up and around. Up? How could that be? Wasn't he on the top floor?

The voices echoed behind him. He had to climb. No choice. Up, right, up, right, up again. Another wall, another turn, spiraling higher and higher. He was utterly out of breath. Should he shout? Call for help? Where was he going? Light flooded in from the left. A french window. A balcony outside. And the most amazing view of Frederik's Hill he had ever seen. Rows of rooftops, the station, the library. The observation tower, recently opened. And now he knew where he was.

"The lighthouse. I'm climbing the lighthouse."

But that was no good. He started back down. And there was the detective's voice again.

He wheeled around. Two stairs at a time, up and

around, legs aching, chest burning, feeling dizzy. Vertigo. Nausea. Another old, arched door. A keyhole. A key sticking out. He turned the knob, but the door was locked. He twisted the key till it clicked, tugged it from the lock, slipped through, and locked it again from the other side. Pressed his ear to the wood and waited. The voices. Close. Right outside. The doorknob rattled.

"Nope," said a detective. "No hippos up here either." And the footsteps receded.

He was in a cramped space at the base of a final spiral of stairs. Overhead, everything was golden. A wash of evening sunshine flooding a vast space. He reached the top and found himself inside an octagonal chamber of glass three times the height of a man.

The gradually setting sun had set the whole horizon on fire, and it filled the space with glare. An enormous searchlight was mounted on a pillar at its heart—and a giant telescope on a giant pole with a set of steps leading up to it.

The mayor's secret watchtower. How often did she stand up here, staring? And which way? Toward Frederik's house? Into his bedroom? Shining her massive light on his private affairs. He shuddered. Up here, it was clear how exposed he had been, had *always* been. The whole of the borough of Frederik's Hill surrounded him, laid out like a map, the golden sunset painting every rooftop, every chimney.

There was another violent shudder and something clattered.

He jumped. Couldn't see anything. Blinded by the sun shining right in his eyes.

Then a silhouette moved across the glare.

A tall, elegant, female silhouette. Straight of back and long of neck. Hair pinned behind in a knot. She turned and stared directly at him.

Frederik thought he might throw up. The mayor was *here*. She must have realized something was wrong when the ground shook. Must have slipped away and headed back to find out what. There was another tremor, but she just stood there, silent, a dark shadow against the flare of the sunset.

Something whizzed into the sky behind her. A firework. There was a faraway crack, and it scattered thousands of multicolored sparks like a blooming flower. She was a dark silhouette, haloed with glaring, golden light and tiny, falling stars.

"Muffin!" she said. "Whatever kept you?"

Club Sandwich

Pernille?" Frederik gasped.

"Expecting someone else?"

"The mayor," he wheezed. "I thought you were the mayor."

Pernille emerged from the golden glow and patted him rather annoyingly on the head. "I'm offended. I thought you'd come to spring me."

"I have! That's why I'm here."

"Well, the mayor is *not* here, I can assure you." She waved a hand in the general direction of the park. "She's over there. I've been watching. She appears to have pulled

things together now, but not long ago she seemed to be having another earthquake."

"She was. That was me."

She leaned her alarming eyes into his face. "*Was* it? How tectonic of you. I told them not to underestimate you. He'll rescue me, I told them."

"Who? Who did you tell?"

"The mayor, the detectives, all of them. I sense I'm starting to irritate them, actually."

"You told the detectives about me? You told the *mayor*?"

"He won't let me down," I said. "Not my little salad sandwich."

"You told them my *name*?"

"Your name isn't salad. Don't be so ridiculous. He'll never stop until I'm free, I told them. Although, I must say, you took longer than I expected."

"I didn't know where you were."

"You didn't see me signaling?"

"No. How could I? You left your pocket penlight behind."

"Did you find it?"

"Well, I did. But then I lost it. In the pipes."

"You *lost* my pocket penlight? How *could* you? Well,

you can go back for it later. It had better not be scratched. Thankfully, I had this massive industrial searchlight to fall back on. You must have seen it, surely? I pointed it straight into your bedroom window."

"The supernova? That was *you*?"

"How many other girls do you have flashlight signal arrangements with?" She seemed rather offended.

"None. But I thought that was the mayor too."

"What would *she* be signaling about? She's been too busy driving me bananas. Up here, day after day, throwing questions around like confetti. Why did you do this, why did you do that, who do you think you are, young lady? But did I buckle? No, I did not. Except for the time she brought cake. But other than that, no. Not once."

"You told her my name!"

"Well," she said. "I could hardly take *all* the credit, could I? You've made an almost equal contribution to my own."

"Almost equal?" he spluttered. "Do you know what I had to do to get here today? Do you know how many rules I've broken?"

"How many?"

"All of them! Every single one."

"Really?" she said. "I'm impressed. Shall we go? Can't stand around chin wagging all day." She started toward the stairs.

"The detectives are down there."

"Mortensen and Martensen? I can handle those two. We've firmly established who wears the pants in that relationship."

"We have to find my parents too. Venkatamahesh is down there, searching."

"He's here?"

"And Rasmus Rasmussen."

"How lovely. The whole club. We need a name, don't you think? Club Sandwich! In honor of you. We can have a midsummer party of our own."

"Speaking of which," he said, "what's happening in the park?"

"Oh, come and see." She flounced headlong into the blaze of sunlight. Frederik followed, blinded.

"Didn't you once have a telescope?" she asked.

"Yes. It was smashed in the earthquake. I miss it."

"Well, try this one for size."

A gray, steel pillar rose ten feet from the floor.

Balanced on the top, precisely weighted, was eight feet of high-powered astronomical telescope. Two smaller tubes ran parallel to the lower end. Viewfinders. Steps led up to the eyepiece.

Pernille sprang up the steps and hauled the telescope in a sweep to point at the park. "It's a super view. You can make out people's individual nostril hairs."

Frederik climbed up and pressed his eye to the disk of brass and glass. Saw a swim of whitish gray. He tugged at the handles and the telescope glided effortlessly. Something yellow wandered by. What was that? He nudged it back. Part of the castle. The western wing, in spectacular detail. It was like he was there. He trained the telescope on the hillside. Picnickers everywhere. He could zoom in on their faces. He could see what they had in their baskets.

He tugged again. More crowds. The boating lake. A duck. A long table on a lawn, candles in silver holders. A man laughing, rosy cheeked. The edge of a stage. The edge of a dress. The edge of an arm, bare to the shoulder. An elegant neck. Pale skin. Prim, white hair, pinned behind. Kamilla Kristensen! Her Ladyship the Mayor. And what was she doing? Chatting and laughing. Animated. Who was she talking to? He nudged the control and moved a fraction of an inch.

"The queen," he breathed. "The mayor is down there talking to the queen."

He tilted the telescope up again and scanned the brow of the ramparts behind the crowd. "Nice job, Calamity."

There had to be one hundred marbles, shoulder to shoulder, along the top of the hill, staring blankly from tricycle buckets and strollers and trolleys and one or two supermarket carts. The picnickers were paying no attention to them, too enthralled by the royal pantomime playing out below.

Another tremor rattled the hill and people looked alarmed, but only briefly. Then they went back to whatever they were eating, as though used to it now.

He pivoted back to the mayor and the queen and a newcomer. A soldier. The soldier laid a box in front of the queen. He lifted something from it. A loop of heavy gold chain with a large, shiny medallion. "What's that?" Frederik wondered.

Pernille took a look. "That is the National Medal for Civic Service. It's to be awarded to the mayor tonight. She's been crowing about it all week. It will make her one of the most prominent politicians in the land."

"We must stop that."

"How?"

"With the giant industrial searchlight?"

The flick of a switch and a yank of a lever. Light erupted from the searchlight. It was terrifically hot and Frederik had to lean his head back, blinking. It took all his strength to swing it around and aim it at the park. The beam tracked across the ramparts of Frederik's Hill, over the enormous crowd.

"Guide me," he told her.

She pressed her eye to the telescope. "Left a bit. Down. Right. No, too far. A little bit left. That's it!"

"What's happening down there?"

"The mayor is shouting a lot and pointing our way and not especially pleased. The queen is trying to shield her eyes with her hat."

"Perfect. That should tie them up for a bit. Now come on. I've got family to find."

They rushed down the stairs, two steps at a time. Out of the lighthouse, onto the sixth floor, fifth floor, fourth.

"Watch for Venkatamahesh," Frederik panted.

"There he is! Mr. Ramasubramanian!"

The disheveled, little shopkeeper hurried along a

hallway, delighted. "Miss Pernille! It is miraculous to see you. If my mother were here—"

"Later," said Frederik, grabbing his arm and hauling him to the stairs. "Did you find my parents?"

"No sign anywhere. Maybe they are in the basement?"

"I don't think so," Frederik said with deep misgivings. "But let's look again." They hurried down the stairs.

"How *are* you, dear man?" Pernille was asking. "Has it been terrible for you?"

"Very distressing, as a matter of fact. My business is ruined."

Pernille gave him a consoling squeeze.

"I never even wanted to be a shopkeeper," he went on. "It is such a pitiful cliché."

"What did you want to be?" she asked.

"Oh, I don't know. Something outdoorsy." He laid a kindly hand on Pernille's elbow and looked up into her enormous eyes. "Did you find your mother?"

"No." She gulped. "Although I found the Department of Unwanted Offspring. It really is hidden away. In fact, it's just a filing cabinet. A tiny handful of cases, and the only pending one is my own." She turned to Frederik. "There's a process underway to cancel my adoption. It just needs the mayor's signature."

"I heard," he said.

"But I found no trace of who I am or where I came from."

"I'm sorry to hear that," said Venkatamahesh.

They hurried down to the second floor, the first, their feet slapping on the tiles, their conversation echoing in the stairwell. Around the final corner.

Two tall detectives in identical suits blocked the way completely. "Well, good evening."

Frederik skidded to a halt just inches from their shiny shoes. Pernille yelped.

Martensen reached out to grab Frederik. "We were heading outside to hunt for you. You saved us the effort."

Frederik shrugged the hand from his shoulder. "Where are my parents?"

"You'll join them soon enough," the detective growled. "You're all going on a journey."

"Where are they? I know they're in this building."

Martensen shook his head. "Wrong. They're not. They're being sent away. And now you're here, we can get on with it."

"Let them go! Let them out!"

Mortensen shrugged. "Can't. Only Her Ladyship can authorize that. And Her Ladyship is busy just now."

And then, right there, at that precise moment, little Venkatamahesh Ramasubramanian, downtrodden and despondent, simply snapped. Popped. Went a tiny bit la-la. He marched up to the two detectives, each of whom was twice his height. He jabbed a stubby finger into the belly of the first, to the detective's utter surprise. He tilted his head back and bellowed. He actually bellowed. Him. Little Mr. Venkatamahesh Ramasubramanian. Right there in the polished hallways of Municipal Hall.

"Stand aside!" he bellowed. "Get out of our way! Who do you think you are, you overgrown bullies?"

Mortensen and Martensen exchanged glances, disconcerted.

"You are servants of the community. Your salaries are paid by the taxpayer. Me! And yet here you stand, impeding my way and that of my juvenile companions."

"We," Mortensen said, recovering, "represent the law, Mr. Submarine."

"My name is *not* Submarine, you ignorant buffoon.

My name is Venkatamahesh Ramasubramanian. If that is too many syllables for your tiny mind, I cannot say I am surprised. But it is my name nonetheless, and if you cannot manage to get it right, I suggest you shut up entirely!"

He shoved Mortensen rather hard into Martensen and attempted to carry on by. It didn't work. Mortensen regained his balance, stretched out a long arm, and pinned Venkatamahesh to the shiny marble wall.

"Leave my friend alone!" Frederik grabbed Venkatamahesh and tried to pull him away from the detective.

Martensen took Frederik by the scruff of the neck, hoisting him almost off his feet.

"No!" Pernille shouted, marching on them in a fury.

And then another unexpected thing occurred.

There was a sudden, enormous crash. The polished floor beneath their feet seemed to skip several inches sideways. Everything started to shake. And then harder. And from somewhere downstairs came the most tremendous roar.

Obstacles

Martensen dropped Frederik like a sack. "What was that noise?"

Mortensen's hand fell away from Venkatamahesh. "The hippo?"

"It came from downstairs. Should one of us look?"

"What about the prisoners?"

"Hold on to them tight." Martensen went jogging to the door marked *Basement*. Opened it carefully, stared down the stairs, ducked his head, and disappeared.

Now there was only one detective left. Farther down the hallway, there was a door marked *Fire Exit*.

"Pernille," Frederik hissed, trying to point with his eyes.

And then, from somewhere down those stairs, there came a bloodcurdling cry of terror.

"Martensen?" said Mortensen, turning pale. He ran to the stairs and peered down. "Are you all right?"

A second awful moan echoed up the staircase, and Mortensen sprinted down. "Wait! I'm coming."

"This way," said Frederik, grabbing Pernille's hand on one side and Venkatamahesh's on the other. They erupted out of the exit, into the sunset.

"We're free!" Pernille cheered. She grabbed Frederik, hugged him hard, and tousled his hair to a tangled mess. "Thank you! Thank you, thank you! I *knew* you'd find me. I never doubted it."

The two of them rushed into the roadway. No cars, no bicycles, no buses, no one. From the direction of the park, there were snatches of music.

"What now?" Frederik said. "Where can we go that's safe?"

"Nowhere is safe." Venkatamahesh was lagging several yards behind. "Nowhere is safe so long as the mayor holds office. She will pursue us to the ends of the land and eject us."

"But we're free!" Pernille said.

"Free of what?" Venkatamahesh wandered across the street toward his shabby convenience store. "I will never be free." He shook his head. "Place your faith in the deities, my mother used to say. Vishnu and Lakshmi and the one with the extra eyes, I can't remember his name. The protector and the destroyer and the remover of obstacles. But where is *my* remover of obstacles? Where is Ganesh? Who will remove *this* obstacle?" He flung an accusing finger toward his shut and shaded store. "This burden! This millstone! How will I ever be rid of it?" He turned and looked Frederik in the eye.

There was silence. No hint of a breeze, no noise, nothing.

And then the road jolted. The windows of the Ramasubramanian Superstore rattled. Venkatamahesh, looking back across the street, opened his eyes extremely wide. His mouth fell open. Frederik turned.

He saw the pavement buckle.

The steps that led beneath Municipal Hall, the entrance to the long-forgotten station, seemed to yawn. The walls around the top collapsed in a rain of broken bricks. The sidewalk shuddered, and from the widening hole, a head appeared. A very large, wrinkled, hairy head. Square ears, black eyes, a trunk, and two enormous, vicious tusks.

The bull elephant rose from the ground with a roar and a crash. He shook the debris from his back and marched into the street, snorting. He stared down at Venkatamahesh.

"Ganesh?" whispered the shopkeeper.

The elephant growled, low and decisive. He walked forward, sending Venkatamahesh scurrying. He leveled the flat of his forehead against the storefront. And kept walking.

The plate-glass window of the Ramasubramanian Superstore folded in and fell with a terrifying crash. Weapons of jagged glass exploded onto the sidewalk. The brickwork above the window gave way and showered over the elephant. The bedroom window cracked and caved in. And the elephant kept walking.

The door popped from its hinges and fell into the street. The doorframe snapped like a twig. Soups and sauces and milk and cheeses were tossed aside. Cereals, vegetables, and cakes were quite destroyed. The bull's back pressed against the ceiling and a furrow of dents and cracks opened up. Plaster fell in handfuls. Beams groaned and gave.

The checkout counter was sliced in two by a tusk.

The water pipes burst. The cash register was upended, and what little change was in it rolled away. The garbage can in the back room tipped, and sour chococcino washed across the floor.

The elephant turned, tearing shelves from walls and walls from one another. The upstairs sagged, the ceiling held up by the elephant's back and nothing more. And as he tore himself from the shell of Venkatamahesh's shop, the upper floors collapsed completely, caved inward, and fell in a cloud of brick dust and broken wood.

The elephant stopped in the street and turned his eyes on Venkatamahesh. He sneezed. Flapped his ears.

The Ramasubramanian Superstore, the apartment above, the students' flat above that, and three more floors of living rooms had been utterly demolished. There was nothing recognizable left standing. Chunks of masonry crumbled and fell to the sidewalk.

Way overhead, the brilliant beam of the searchlight lanced from the lighthouse into the heart of the Garden Park. There was a faraway thud, and silver fireworks exploded in the darkening sky. A chorus of crackles. Distant cheers. Blue stars, orange stars.

The huge bull elephant stamped his feet and the roadway shuddered some more. And then, from the hole in the ground by Municipal Hall, his sisters and wives and daughters emerged one by one. And Rasmus Rasmussen. And one of the detectives. The detective was extremely dusty. He sat down in the street and stared at the gap where the store had been.

Venkatamahesh was staring too. A hesitant smile was playing at the corners of his mouth.

"Padma!" Rasmus was heading briskly toward the setting sun. "Renuka!"

The bull elephant had marched away toward the pond and the blue house and the yellow. The others were following, saggy behinds silhouetted against the glare, fireworks popping and bursting overhead.

"Come back!" called Rasmus. "Oh boy. This is going to be hard to explain." He broke into an ungainly jog, trying to catch them before they demolished anything else.

"What fun," said Pernille.

"I still haven't found my parents," Frederik blurted. "Where can they be?"

He stared at the ruined shop and the enormity of it all

caught up with him. He had triggered an earthquake and a flood, stolen the mayor's marbles, and wrecked the underside of Municipal Hall. He'd sprung two prisoners, assaulted a detective, and destroyed conspicuous real estate directly outside the mayor's window. And what had he imagined would happen next? He hadn't. He hadn't thought about it. He'd been so intent on rescuing everyone that what happened next had seemed irrelevant.

But he couldn't just go home and hope it all blew over. He was the greatest, most prolific breaker of rules in the history of Frederik's Hill. He turned to Pernille. "The mayor will never forgive us. She'll hunt us down with every resource she has."

"Then we will stop her," Pernille said. "Now. Right now. She's a hypocrite. A liar. We must bring her down once and for all. We must stop her canceling my adoption. We must stop her deporting your parents. We must stop her. Forever."

Frederik took a deep breath. "There might be a way."

"I knew we'd think of something. We always do, you and I."

They ran across the street, past the parking lot, the

pond, and the never-open gallery. The gates of the Garden Park were dead ahead. But shut! Padlocked. A sign: *Special event. No admittance.* Pernille leapt at the fence. Used her long legs to clamber up and over the top. She hung there, swaying more than six feet in the air. She grabbed Frederik's hand and hauled him up. He teetered at the top, about to topple, somehow got his balance, dropped into the park.

They sped toward the canal and the door in the floor. Fireworks clattered overhead. The sound of the crowd and the orchestra beyond the trees. And once again, the feeling that the ground was not quite right. Ripples in the subsoil, tremors in their shoes.

"What's causing all this shaking?" she panted.

"Me. I was back at the..."

And then he paused.

In front of them, in weird slow motion, the door in the floor was rising into the air. It hovered five feet above the ground. And then, like a cork from a champagne bottle, it flew into the sky, propelled by a thundering eruption of Volcanade.

"...brewery," he added.

"*You* did this?"

"Yes."

"For me?"

"Yes."

She gave him an unexpected hug. "I *love* it."

They galloped along the edge of the canal, fireworks reflected in the water. They hurried over bridges and lawns, rushed through rushes and trees, and there, dead ahead, was the catering marquee, stacked with fancy foods on fancy platters. The castle ramparts beyond, crowded with almost every resident of the borough. The bonfire raft in the boating lake was ablaze, splashing reds and vivid oranges into the deep-blue evening. Her Ladyship the Mayor's International Midsummer Festival.

A Selection of Very Bad Things

They crept through the shadows to the back of the stage. The VIP table faced out to the hillside. There were foreign dignitaries, members of the government, and center stage, lit up by the blinding beam of the lighthouse searchlight, sat Her Ladyship the Mayor and Her Majesty the Queen, side by side, exchanging chitchat, raising a toast.

Another shudder swept underfoot. There were gasps from the hillside. Heads turned at the head table.

The mayor bent to the queen and whispered something. She slid her chair back and stood. Her dress was an elegant

blue, her arms bare. There was a microphone on a stand. "Goodness me," she told the crowd in a jovial tone. "Aren't these little vibrations fun? All part of the show, I assure you. All planned. Nothing to worry about."

"She's lying to them all," said Frederik. "Like always. She hasn't planned any such thing."

But as though she had, in a sudden sweep from left to right, nine magnificent fountains erupted from the boating lake. A layer of lemony fizzing froth settled on the surface of the water. Volcanade. The crowd *ooh*ed and *aah*ed.

The mayor yelped and lost her thread, but only for a moment. She gripped the microphone, improvising brilliantly. "May I present the newly restored and long missed fountains of Frederik's Hill!" And a roar of approval echoed down from the crowd.

"I don't *believe* it," spat Pernille. "She's getting away with this. They like her more than ever. They'll swallow *anything* she tells them."

The foreign dignitaries rose to give the mayor a standing ovation. The queen got slowly to her feet.

"This has to *stop*," Pernille wailed.

The queen reached for the microphone. The audience

hushed, dazzled by the fire, the fountains, and the mayor's finest moment.

"Ladies and gentlemen," the queen said, her small voice relayed across the hillside by hundreds of high-fidelity speakers. "What a wonderful evening. Allow me to congratulate Her Ladyship the Mayor of Frederik's Hill."

Frederik and Pernille clambered up the back of the stage. The searchlight threw the surrounding lawns into deep shadow. No one could see them. Not yet. But soon. When they crossed into that pool of brilliant light. They would have to be quick. They would have to be like lightning. But what exactly would they do?

"Kamilla Kristensen," said the queen, "has proved herself a champion of our little nation."

Frederik stayed low, keeping to the shadows, feeling extraordinarily exposed with thousands of people staring at the women just in front of him. Pernille grabbed his arm. "What's the plan?" she hissed.

"I haven't got a plan."

"We need a plan."

"I know we need a plan."

"Then make one."

"*You* make one!"

"I don't know."

"Neither do I!"

The queen held up the medal for all to see. "And it gives me such pleasure to present Her Ladyship Kamilla Kristensen, tonight, right now, before you all, with the National Medal for Civic Service."

The mayor dipped her head. The queen draped the chain over her shoulders. The mayor turned to the microphone.

"Thank you," she said. "I am so—"

"*Where* are my *parents*?"

Frederik would forever after wonder why he did it. There was no conscious decision. No thought process. He simply stood tall, ran at high speed into the glare of the spotlight in front of thousands of people, and shouted. At the mayor. In front of the queen.

The effect, to be fair, was impressive.

For starters, the mayor did not get to enjoy her moment of glory. And that, without doubt, was a good thing. It was perhaps the only good thing, however. And it was directly accompanied by a selection of very bad things.

For example, the three elite palace guardsmen who

pounced in a heartbeat on top of Frederik's head. Also, the posse of TV people who swung into Frederik's field of vision and stayed there, pointing their cameras at him. Then there was the glimpse of Pernille, sailing awkwardly through the air and landing on the dining table in front of the queen.

Pernille grabbed the microphone, stood on the table, completely ignored the gathered officials, and addressed the enormous crowd.

"Ahem," she said. "Well. Yes. Good evening."

There was a howl of feedback and everyone winced. A security guard was moving rapidly toward her, reaching out a massive hand. Frederik grabbed the guard's ankle. He toppled like a bowling pin and sprawled under the table. The queen shrieked, and another heavily armed soldier was deployed, this time in entirely the wrong direction, and became wedged between some chairs in full ceremonial uniform.

"Get down off that table," the mayor was shrieking. "Get down at once! How did *you* get *here*?"

"This whole event," Pernille announced, at booming, echoing volume, "is a sham!"

A gasp swept the crowd.

"The mayor is not who she seems!" Pernille was

gaining confidence, getting louder. "She is a fake! A fraud! She has duped us for years. Nothing she says can be trusted. She is despicable. Disgraceful." She paused. To assess her impact. To see who was with her.

But even from his cramped position, head pressed to the floor, and several troops of the household cavalry sitting on him, Frederik could see who was with her.

No one.

The foreign VIPs were whispering outrage. The folk of Frederik's Hill were staring, shocked and ashamed, at the girl on the table, embarrassing the mayor, embarrassing the queen, embarrassing everyone.

And then Pernille realized too. Her shoulders slumped. Frederik wanted desperately to reach her but couldn't.

A storm of security guards and police arrived all at the same time. Pernille was hoisted off her feet, off the table, and off the stage.

The mayor retrieved the microphone and stood tall, in all her finery, thrusting her chin out at the voters, summoning the political skills that had won election after election. "A graphic example," she declared, "of why we need controls on foreigners in our borough."

"She was born right here!" Frederik shouted, but no one heard, and a soldier jabbed him in the ribs.

"With *all* due respect to our assembled overseas guests," the mayor purred, "we must ensure that malcontents from other lands are rooted out and *ejected*." She breathed the word with chilling malice. The crowd nodded and applauded.

The mayor turned to the queen. "Your Majesty, this is a reminder of the plots against your realm. I volunteer to deal with them. All of them."

The queen was nodding too, regaining her calm. "Yes, well, that might be necessary, I suppose."

The mayor smiled.

"Your Worthyship! Hey! Down there! Your Worthyship!"

The voice was brash, brusque, and it came from high on the hillside. The soldiers got up to look, releasing the pressure from Frederik's head. He peered between the queen's legs. The crowd on the hillside was parting down the middle, like a gangway. And weaving down the gangway, rosy face lit up by the bonfire, was Henrik Hotdog.

"Here they are, Your Worthyship!" he shouted. "We brought them all." And he cackled out loud to the dismay of respectable citizens.

"Be *quiet*!" the mayor retorted. "Security? Where are you?" They were mostly right behind her, sitting on Frederik and Pernille.

Henrik Hotdog was approaching the foot of the hillside now and the edge of the boating lake. Picnickers and party-goers drew back from him, horrified. A man attempted to challenge him but earned a firm shove in the chest.

"Sorry we're late!" Henrik shouted. "There were loads of the bloody things. Took us ages."

"What *things*?" the mayor spat, crackling with anger.

"Them horrible things up there!" Henrik replied, and he pointed to the top of the slope.

Frederik wriggled till he could see. There were thousands of festival goers, all across the hillside, in summer dresses and shorts and party hats. Their faces flickered orange with the firelight. On top of the hill was the yellow face of the castle, the national flag flapping above its green copper roof. And between the back of the crowd and the front of the castle, a line of gray faces stared coldly down the hill. Chilling, stone statues positioned side by side across the brim of the steep ramparts. Hundreds of them, ingeniously mounted on anything with wheels.

"My marbles," the mayor breathed, aghast.

"Is that what you call them, Your Worthiness? Bloody heavy is what I call them." And Henrik cackled out loud again. "Anyway. Glad to be of service." He turned to the crowd. "Who's for hot dogs? See me at the cart at the top of the hill. Special festival prices. Only fifty percent higher than usual."

"Wait!" the mayor spluttered. "What?" She seemed unable to process the sight of the statues at the top of the slope.

"I recognize those," said the queen, craning to stare across the crowd.

"Ah," said the mayor. "I can explain."

"Some of them are from my palace. They went missing. Years ago."

"Yes!" the mayor said. "And I found them. Restored them for you."

"They don't look very restored."

"She's lying!" Frederik wailed from the floor.

The crowds on the hillside were confused. Few could see the marbles above and behind them. Too many people in the way.

"Bring them forward," the queen instructed. "Whoever is up there, bring them forward."

For a moment, nothing happened. And then, Calamity Claus appeared. He took hold of a statue in a stroller, and he hauled it to the very edge of the hill where everyone could see it. But just at the critical moment, something seemed to catch his eye. He let go of the stroller and pointed down the hillside, past the lake, and somewhere beyond Frederik's head.

"Oooh!" he exclaimed at the top of his voice. "Look down there! An elephant!"

Only You

All across the hillside, people started pointing and snapping pictures. "Elephants! Ooh, aren't they big?"

The palace guards were looking and pointing too, and a little less calmly. "Elephants! Get the queen to the car."

"No!" the mayor shrilled above the hubbub. "Nonsense, Your Majesty. This is all part of our planned entertainment. Our fabulous fountains, the newly restored marbles. And what festival would be complete without an elephant or two?"

"Or possibly seven," said a soldier. "Heading this way. Get the queen out of here!"

From the deepening darkness behind the stage, a figure came suddenly running, waving his arms, belly bouncing and face all red. Rasmus Rasmussen. He scrambled up the back of the stage and collapsed across the dining table, knocking over a glass of wine and staining his sleeve with marinara sauce.

"Slight problem!" he croaked. "Nothing I can't handle. Just need to..." And then his eyes locked on something out beyond the crowd.

Something at the top of the hill.

"Oh no," Frederik breathed. "Oh no."

"*Zombies!*" Rasmus howled like a wounded animal. He shoved the table aside, tipping several dignitaries off their chairs. Grabbed the microphone. Yelled. "Zombies! The zombies are here! They're behind you! Run! Run!"

The International Midsummer Festival had hardly gone flawlessly up till then. Several events entirely unmentioned in the official program had caught everyone by surprise. But none of them quite as surprising as this. After weeks of chatter and twitter and rumor, the folk of Frederik's Hill were all too ready to believe in the presence of the undead. That became clear as they moved, almost as one, very rapidly down the hill, piling up on the brink of the boating lake, terrified faces frozen in the firelight, fountains gushing Volcanade twenty feet in the air, and fireworks raining tiny, golden stars from the darkening heavens.

"Zombies!" Rasmus hollered again and again. "Zombies are coming!"

At the top of the hill, Calamity Claus was just as alarmed as anyone. The marble he'd brought forward got away and started rolling. One by one, jogged and shoved by the fleeing public, the other bicycles and tricycles and skateboards and baby carriages tipped lazily over the edge and followed it down the hillside.

And now, the screams were coming from the grassy banks themselves, as adults and children, young and old, scrambled in horror from the path of hundreds of hideous, glaring figures cascading down toward the boating lake.

"Zombies! Run! Save us! Help!"

And then the back of the stage was crushed under the foot of a vast shadow looming out of the night. The head table was swept aside, and the dignitaries were floored once more by the lash of a massive tusk with a brass cap. The bull elephant roared, wrecked the stage, and marched on the boating lake, his little herd at his heels.

"Help! Elephants!" people were wailing.

"Help! Zombies!" screamed everyone else.

The ground was shuddering and lurching yet again. The elephants tore through the catering marquee. They leveled it. Flattened it. The roof fell in, enveloping trifles and tarts in giant folds of canvas. Gretchen Grondal, hobnobbing by the buffet and trying to re-ingratiate herself, was tipped headfirst into a mound of cream and crushed meringue. And the elephants kept going. Down the grassy bank to the edge of the lake. Into the water.

From the other side came hundreds of people, wading up to their thighs and scaring the ducks and holding their babies over their heads. And right behind, bearing down on them, ugly, grimacing gargoyles made of stone: The mayor's marbles. Rasmus's zombies. The cause of it all. The cause of everything. Thirty years of lies. The forgotten, sneering faces of Kamilla Kristensen's greed.

"Pernille," Frederik gasped, getting somehow to his feet. The guards were all preoccupied now, with the elephants and statues and general public racing headlong toward collision in the lake. "Pernille, where are you?"

Everything was chaos. There were floodlights swinging

wildly about and fireworks flashing in the sky and the bonfire roaring out of control at the heart of the lake, its light refracted in the fountains of pop. Faces appeared and disappeared in shadow again. Bodies flailing everywhere. He couldn't make out who was who. "Pernille!" he shouted. "Pernille!"

And then he saw her.

Or did he?

What was he seeing? Was he seeing double?

The beam of the lighthouse searchlight still bore down on what was left of the stage. Standing at its center, a dark silhouette against the bright-white glare, Pernille. Clearly Pernille. Hands on hips. A halo of pure-white hair about her head. Tall. Willowy. Defiant.

Staring. Angrily. Furiously.

At herself. Pernille. Another identical silhouette. Hands on hips. A halo of pure-white hair. Tall and willowy and haughty, staring, angry.

"What?" he murmured. "Wait." Which was which? Pernille and Pernille? Was he out of his mind? Had he banged his head?

The two Pernilles were shouting, both of them, leaning forward, hurling abuse at each other from close quarters in almost identical ways. Same stance, same gestures, same frame, same build, same height, everything. And then they both threw their hands in the air in rage and backed away, glaring, snarling, and one of them, sure enough—as the angle changed and the light broke and Frederik could finally see—*was* Pernille.

And the other was not.

It was the mayor.

It was Kamilla Kristensen.

Pernille's captor. Pernille's nemesis. Pernille's…

"*Mama,*" Frederik breathed. "She *is* Pernille's mama!"

A cacophony of rockets exploded hundreds of feet above the stage, and the evening was suddenly day for the briefest instant, color raining about them all. Illuminating a soup of people, floundering and panicking in the boating lake, waist deep, crying out in dismay. A brigade of sneering statues, bowling into the water, their momentum abruptly checked. Some tipping and splashing sideways, others standing staring out of the lake like zombies; just like zombies. And a broadside of broad backsides, as elephant after elephant thrashed through the water to meet them.

The noise was terrific. It was a riot of flashes and

glimpses and horror. The elephants met the marbles maybe ten feet from the edge. They didn't pause for a moment. They crashed through the water and they crashed through the statues, wave upon wave of them, sinking them deep underwater, driving them backward into the bank, trampling, crushing, pulverizing every single one. Grinding the mayor's marbles into a powder that drifted like smoke on the evening air.

"Stop!" the mayor howled into the microphone. "Stop them!"

A long, black limousine slid to the side of the stage in a heck of a hurry. Her Majesty the Queen was bundled to the open door, and the car sped away across the lawns.

"No!" yelled the mayor. "Come back!"

Henrik Hotdog's hot dog cart was trundling uncontrolled down the hillside, veering side to side, threatening to run over anyone who got in the way. Henrik Hotdog waddled twenty yards behind it, out of control himself, running and tumbling down the steep slope.

A giant figure wandered to the very front of the stage, staring out across the chaos, rubbing his head in confusion. It was Rasmus. Frederik ran to his side. They watched the herd of elephants climb the hill, scattering the remaining onlookers and trampling statues into the lawn.

"You!" the mayor roared. She stormed across the stage, microphone in hand, and started hitting Rasmus with it. Muffled thuds echoed across the park. "You cretin!" she roared. "You moron! You miserable excuse for a man. You scum. You vandal. Look what you've done to my *glory*! *My* glory!"

"Me?" Rasmus said, grabbing her arm and holding her microphone hand in the air so she couldn't batter him anymore. "Me?"

"You! Always you! Only you! Every time I'm on the brink, there you are. In the way. Ruining everything!" The National Medal for Civic Service slipped from her shoulders and pinned her arms to her sides like a lasso. She couldn't move them. She staggered around like a penguin, threw her head back, and roared with rage. The chain slipped farther and jammed at her elbows.

Frantic people were running in every direction, yelling, pleading for help. Clambering up the slick banks of the lake on hands and knees, their clothing saturated, caught between helping their loved ones and saving themselves.

The mayor took a step too far and toppled off the edge of the stage. There was a gasp. Frederik held his breath. And then there was a squelch and a screech of revulsion. He slithered to the lip and looked down.

Her Ladyship the Mayor had landed in the middle of a mound of elephant dung. It broke her fall and no doubt prevented her breaking anything else. But she didn't seem to appreciate her luck. She was howling, wailing. Arms still pinned motionless by her medal chain.

Rasmus jumped down and helped her to sit. Steaming green doo-doo all over her elegant, sleeveless gown. All over her arms. On her face. In her mouth. She spat and retched.

Rasmus squatted at her side and tried to remove the chain, the microphone still cradled under his arm.

"What have you *done*?" she screamed at him. "Do you know the lengths I had to go to? Burying the past, silencing dissent, making all the mindless morons who live in this borough do exactly as I say. Do you think that was easy? Do you think that was cheap? Do you think I'll let you blunder back into my life with your disgusting creatures and smash it all up again? *Again?* I should have dealt with you properly the first time, but no! I was weak. I was sentimental. Well, never again!"

She drew the deepest of breaths, gasped as the chain tightened around her midriff.

"This time," she hissed, "I will make you disappear for good. You and those horrid foreign kids with their skin and their idiotic accents. *Don't* think I can't. I've done it before, and I'll do it again! I'll wipe every memory of you away, and no one will know you existed! I will erase you like I erased the railway, like I erased the earthquake. Like all who dare disrupt me. Like unwanted offspring. I will not be stopped! I will not have my reputation sullied by you! I *never* knew you! We were *never* an item. You're *nothing* to me! You're a disgusting lowlife and I'm going to make you *disappear*!"

She stared, incensed, at Rasmus.

His shadow was a broad, black line stretching out to the lake. A long, black shadow in the searing light.

And then she realized.

The searchlight was shining directly on them both. On Rasmus and her. The searchlight and the TV cameras. And Rasmus had the microphone under his arm. And the finest firework display ever seen on Frederik's Hill had finally ended. And everyone, in every direction, had stopped screaming and running around and had turned to stare.

At the mayor. And it was very, very quiet across the Royal Garden Park. Save for the last echoes of her voice across the hillside, broadcast loud and clear to everyone by the highly expensive high-fidelity public-address system.

"You and I are *finished*!" she spat at Rasmus, unable to stop her bitterness spilling to the surface one last time, like bile.

Rasmus Rasmussen stared at Her Ladyship the Mayor from the depths of an infinite sadness.

"No," he said. "Only you."

One Week After Her Ladyship the Mayor's Unforeseeable Midsummer Debacle

An oak tree reached its canopy of leaves over the pond and the grass. Frederik stretched his legs from a bench in sun-dappled shade. They failed to reach anywhere near as far as Pernille's. A block away, a digger was shoveling remains of the Ramasubramanian Superstore onto the back of a truck.

"This must be difficult to watch," Frederik said to Venkatamahesh.

The little man sat beside Pernille. He laughed. "Not at all."

"But aren't you ruined?" Pernille asked.

The former shopkeeper smiled. "Actually, no. After the earthquake, some months back, I used what little cash remained to buy some insurance. I thought it wise. Today, I received a check. Also, a windfall payment from the Borough of Frederik's Hill. It seems they are keen for me to keep quiet about last Friday's incident."

"But what will you do, now that your business is gone?"

"Something new," he said. "Maybe something with wildlife. I have experience, after all."

Frederik spotted a familiar figure mounting a bicycle outside Municipal Hall.

"Father!" he called as the cyclist drew close. "Over here!"

Father braked, grinned, waved, collided with a lamppost. Wheeled his wobbly bicycle onto the green and shook Venkatamahesh's hand.

"You and your wife had a narrow escape," said Venkatamahesh.

"We did," said Father. "They had us in the back of a van, ready to go to the airport."

"And now?"

"Now they are very apologetic."

"I bet."

The four of them ambled down the street together, past the blue house and the yellow, toward home.

"Any more news from Municipal Hall?" Frederik asked.

"They're doing a lot of what's called *damage limitation,*" Father explained. "It means making up iffy excuses."

Frederik had some of those prepared too. Even now, one week after the dust had cleared, quite literally, from Her Ladyship the Mayor's unforeseeable midsummer debacle, he found it stunning that he hadn't been named, blamed, shamed, or even very much questioned about his appearances on national TV in the middle of mayhem.

"And the mayor is gone?" asked Venkatamahesh.

"Long gone," said Father. "On what they're calling a *sabbatical.* An *indefinite* sabbatical." He smiled. "She won't be back. She's finished. The brewery is suing her. International investors are abandoning Frederik's Hill. The government is having to offer discounts to keep their business. And the queen is furious about the statues from her palace. She took the medal back."

"What about the zombies?" asked Venkatamahesh. "I still hear people talking about zombies."

"The official position," Father said, "is there are no zombies. Never were. But as you know, thousands of eyewitnesses were sent fleeing in fear, and they are proving hard to persuade. Many believe the mayor set zombies on them, and it was only the elephants that saved them from an appalling death."

"And they're not looking for anyone *else* to blame?" Pernille asked, checking. "Only the mayor?"

"Oh, I didn't say that," said Father. "In fact, the investigation now centers on two individuals thought to have let the elephants out on the street."

Pernille grabbed Frederik's wrist entirely too hard.

"Believe it or not," Father went on, "they're detectives. Names of Martensen and Mortensen. Apparently, they scared the animals onto the road. The rest"—he gestured at the rubble being cleared from Frederik's Avenue—"is history."

The upholsterer stepped from his workshop to greet them in the sunshine. "Mr. Sandwich! And Mr. Ramasubramanian. Frederik, Pernille. How splendid. Can I interest you in coffee?"

Frederik glanced across to the Café Grondal. Its tables stood empty, as they had since the sugar incident. There was no sign of the owner.

"Not over *there,*" the upholsterer said. "Dreadful woman. I make my own these days." He draped an arm around Pernille's shoulders. "We don't talk to her, do we?"

Pernille smiled. "She's no friend of ours. Or relative."

"No!" Frederik agreed. And then he shut up. Had he sounded too certain? Had he given himself away? He hadn't found a way to tell Pernille what he'd seen in the dark and the flashing lights. Pernille and the mayor, silhouetted, indistinguishable from one another. It was coincidence, he kept telling himself. A trick of the light. The stress.

"I've given up my search," Pernille said to her papa. "It's time. You're the only parent I need."

The upholsterer's eyes glistened for a moment. "I'm glad."

"Me too. The whole time I was locked up, all I could think about was getting home to you."

Frederik's father turned to Venkatamahesh. "Things still look bad for Rasmus Rasmussen. He brought those elephants out of the zoo. Heads will roll, and I think it will be his."

"Rasmus Rasmussen is a hero!" insisted Pernille's papa. "My customers say his elephants saved their lives."

"Hero or not," said Father, "he's suspended, pending dismissal. Unless someone comes forward with something convincing, he'll need a new career."

"No!" Frederik yelped.

"We must find him," said Pernille. "Right away."

"I'm coming too," said Venkatamahesh. "I owe that man a debt of infinite gratitude."

The doors of the old, abandoned elephant house were wide open to the fresh air for the first time in many moons. They found Rasmus rifling through papers in a grubby, little office. He was hot and harassed and murmuring words that cannot be repeated. There were people everywhere.

"Go away," he snapped. "I'm busy."

"The whole zoo is busy," Pernille said.

"Thousands of people every day," Rasmus complained. "Busloads of them. They all want to see the elephants."

"But surely that's good?" Frederik said.

"Maddening. People traipsing through my house all day."

"Why are they in your house?" Frederik watched a gaggle of tourists, wandering through the old elephant house, snapping selfies. They headed for the archway that led down to the railway, far beneath.

"Secret's out," said Rasmus. "Everyone wants a walk in the dark to a railway that doesn't go anywhere."

"What precisely are you doing?" Pernille asked, examining the riot of paperwork on the desk and the chair and the shelf and the floor.

"Hunting for my resumé. Haven't needed it for forty years."

Frederik felt awful. He had tricked Rasmus into helping him, and now Rasmus had lost his job. He hid his shame in a folder of papers: *Zoo Rules and Regulations*. Instructions from more than a century of superintendents and mayors. Safety guidelines and employment conditions. Maintenance agreements and feeding schedules. He found an order from Kamilla Kristensen, and a second and a third. Wads of them. Demanding this and that in the most officious tone.

"They'll reinstate you, Rasmus," said Pernille.

"They won't. I shouldn't have let the elephants out of the zoo."

Frederik stared at the folder. *Rules for animal quarantine in the event of outbreak*. And something struck him.

"What is it, muffin?" asked Pernille. "You've had a brainwave. I know that look."

"Help Rasmus," Frederik told her. "There's something I need to do." And he galloped from the elephant house and up through the crowds to the street.

He was back, breathless, in forty-seven minutes. The papers were deeper than ever on the floor. Rasmus was despondent. Pernille was trying to keep his spirits up. Venkatamahesh was peering at small print through large spectacles.

Frederik picked up the folder. He waited till no one was looking, unclipped the rings, hooked an extra sheet of paper inside, and never said a word. Then he shoved the folder at Rasmus and said, "Look! Does this help?"

The other three examined the page, stamped at the top with the crest of Frederik's Hill.

Evacuation of Animals, it said. *I, Kamilla Kristensen, Mayor of Frederik's Hill, hereby order that in an emergency or natural disaster, the animals of the zoo are to be evacuated immediately. By their designated keepers. To Municipal Hall. For safekeeping. By train.*

"Amazingly," Frederik said, "it seems you did exactly what the rules require."

Pernille gave him a long, searching look. "Yes.

Amazingly. And fancy it turning up just at the moment we need it most." She smiled to herself.

"What a relief," said Venkatamahesh. "You are in the clear, Mr. Rasmussen. You are vindicated. Exonerated."

"What about the festival?" Rasmus said. "I'm responsible for seven elephants marauding through a public event. Can't argue otherwise."

"*I* can argue otherwise," insisted Venkatamahesh. "And I will! I was there. I saw those detectives chase them onto the street. I saw your efforts to steer them away from the crowds. Was it your fault a jet of soda pop erupted from the door in the floor and startled them? No. Was it your fault that fountains exploded and statues cascaded down the hill, leading to a general breakdown in public orderliness? No! Was any of this in the mayor's advertised program of events? No! So whose fault was it?"

Frederik coughed.

"The mayor's!" said Venkatamahesh. "You followed protocols to the letter, sir. Your conduct was exemplary. You saved buildings and lives. You saved the queen! And I shall say so. I shall tell them. Believe me, they're keen to keep me sweet."

Rasmus scratched his stubbly chin, somewhat reassured. Venkatamahesh made a pot of tea. It didn't smell quite right, but they were all too thirsty to care. Strangers trailed through the elephant house, videoing. Frederik and his friends ignored them. And that was why they failed to notice the woman at the door until she cleared her throat and knocked.

"What now?" Rasmus barked.

"Oh," she said. "Sorry, dears. Am I interrupting?"

"Edna!" Pernille grabbed the conductor's hand and hauled her through the door. "Tea? Or at least I think it's tea. You know Mr. Ramasubramanian, of course. And Mr. Rasmussen. Excuse his filthy clothes. He's a working man, or very soon will be again, we hope, all being well, fingers crossed."

"I heard about that," said Edna. She straightened her hat. "Have they made you the scapegoat, Rasmus? They do that."

"We have a plan," Frederik said. "Venkatamahesh to the rescue."

"Splendid," said Edna. "The elephants need a keeper who knows what's what." She gave Rasmus the warmest of smiles, and he seemed to suddenly lose his composure. He spilled his tea over his knee.

"But I imagine it may take time to sort things out?" she went on.

"It might do, madam, yes," Rasmus croaked, uncharacteristically bashful. "Some weeks perhaps. Bureaucracy."

"Excellent." She smiled.

"Is it?"

"I don't know if you've heard," she said, "but the uptick in visitors to the zoo is too much for the buses. The borough, what's left of it, has decided to recommission the Municipal Underground Branch Line."

"The Twist?"

"The Twist. But we've got a lot of patching up to do. There's soda in the Cisterns, a mess at Municipal Hall, and the elephant carriage is wrecked."

"Sorry about that," mumbled both Rasmus and Frederik at the same time.

"I was thinking," Edna went on, "who better to supervise repairs than a local man? A man who finds himself temporarily unemployed. A man who knows all there is to know about elephant transportation." The pitch of her voice had gradually risen, and now she sounded silly and self-conscious. She blushed and broke off.

Rasmus shuddered. "Underground? I don't know about that. No, I'm not sure about that."

Edna, crestfallen, backed to the door, not meeting his eye. "Well, think about it anyway. Train leaves in ten minutes. All aboard." She turned away, heading to her lonely railway by herself.

"A job!" hissed Pernille. "Take the job!"

"I don't like it," said Rasmus.

"What? *Why?* I'm honestly *furious* with you, Rasmus. There's nothing down there. No zombies, no statues. You saw them crushed to pieces with your own eyes."

Rasmus stared at Pernille, an extra flush to his blotchy cheeks. "It isn't that."

"What is it, then?"

He coughed and looked away. "It's that lady."

"Which lady?"

"The little one with the hat. I'm frightened I'll make a fool of myself."

Pernille and Frederik leapt in the air. They grabbed Rasmus Rasmussen with no regard for hygiene. They bundled him through the door and the hall and down the ramp to the underground railway.

"Hurry," Frederik told him. "Don't miss that train, whatever you do."

"And whatever you do," Pernille instructed, waving a finger in his face, "be sure to make a fool of yourself with all possible haste!"

Misfitting

In the modest warmth of a summer's day way up there in the north, Frederik and Pernille walked together among the trees and canals of the Royal Garden Park. The grassy hillside below the castle was fenced off. Volunteers were filling in the gouges in the lawn. Wheelbarrows stood by, loaded with what remained of the statues and the last piles of dung. The boating lake was closed, the fountains re-decommissioned.

But a great many things were entirely unchanged on Frederik's Hill. The ducks still bobbed and waddled in everyone's way. The herons stood at the edge of the water, still

as sinister statues, waiting to strike. Parents trundled baby carriages along the quiet paths. Toddlers lurched across the lawns and fell face-first in the daisies.

"There's something I can't help wondering," said Pernille. "Something that doesn't add up."

"Oh? What's that?"

"The mayor had me secretly seized and imprisoned. She visited me every day. Peppered me with questions of an accusatory and rather personal nature—*who* do I think I am, and *what* did I think I was doing, and *who* raised me to be so ill-mannered, and things like that. On and on. And yet, she never once asked about you, muffin. Why on earth not?"

"I've no idea," said Frederik, feeling suddenly very prickly.

"It was almost as if she has some personal issue with me, personally. Why would that be?"

"Don't know. Can't imagine. Can't see any reason at all."

But he could. He could see it as clear as day, or rather night. A wild, chaotic night, with a searchlight searing down on Pernille and the mayor, throwing them both into dark silhouette, side by side, face-to-face, nose to nose and shouting. And, just for that moment, identical.

"It's a mystery," she said.

He couldn't say a word. It would do so much harm. She had finally stopped searching. She was finally at peace.

"Should we investigate?" she said.

"Maybe not. Try to forget it."

Pernille nodded. "You're probably right."

Dead ahead, a band of sullen children skulked on a footbridge.

"Look who it is!" called Erik the Awkward. "The weirdos."

Erica Engel, Erik the Awkward, Frederik Dahl Dalby. Calamity Claus too. He had sustained an ankle sprain, a concussion, and a cauliflower ear on the evening of the festival. Barely a part of him remained unbandaged.

They peeled from the railings and drifted down to the pathway, blocking the route.

"Hi, Calamity," Frederik said. "Fallen into bad company again?"

"No," said Claus. "But I can't limp fast enough to shake them off."

"Where are you going?" Dahl Dalby wanted to know. "This park is for local people."

"We're going exactly wherever we want," Frederik answered back.

"Like elephants," added Pernille.

"Elephants?" said Calamity, panicky. "Again?"

"You had something to do with all of that," said Dahl Dalby. "You were on TV."

Frederik stared back at him. Considered. Decided. "I did. I planned it all—the elephants, the zombies, the earthquake, the flood, and a jailbreak too. I had a busy evening."

The neighbors stared at him, squinting, uncertain.

"Rubbish," said Erica.

"Impossible," said Dahl Dalby.

"Keep this quiet," Frederik whispered, "but Pernille, Claus, and I are to blame for the downfall of the mayor."

"You *can't* be," Erica hissed.

"You're just kids!" said Erik.

"And misfits," said Frederik.

"And we'll thank you," Pernille said, "to keep your noses out of our misfitting."

"You can't talk to us like that," Dahl Dalby threatened.

Pernille and Frederik faced him side by side, shoulder to elbow. Nothing menacing, simply the confidence to stand their ground and say nothing more.

"There are rules on this Hill!" Dahl Dalby insisted, red in the face and somewhat losing his nerve.

"Rules are for fools," Frederik said.

"And I expect," said Pernille, "that *you* will therefore find them useful. But *we*"—and she draped one long arm around Frederik's shoulders and the other around Calamity Claus—"Club Sandwich, do not."

A last stretch of lawn and a stand of trees separated them from the park gate and home. A small, metal sign announced *Keep Off the Grass, By Order of Her Ladyship the Mayor.*

"Shall we, muffin?" Pernille said.

"Certainly, Miss Adventure," he replied.

And arm in arm, their nasty neighbors watching with open mouths, Frederik Sandwich, Calamity Claus, and Pernille Yasemin Jensen marched cheerfully and deliberately across the forbidden lawn, heading for the gate and the tall house by the chimney and the sat-upon roof at the end of the nearby street.

Acknowledgments

Frederik's stories were inspired by the delightfully peculiar people of Denmark.

Thank you to the upper elementary students at Montessori Children's House, Redmond: Aamina, Abbey, Aiden, Alex, Andi, Andreas, Arjun, Claire B., Claire H., Collin, Gage, Gavin, Harloe, JJ, Justin, Kai, Lizzy, Louisa, Lukas, Mason, Max, Miles, Oscar, Payton, Piper, Sabrina, Shaylee, Sophia, and Sophie, and your brilliant teachers, Nicole Champoux and Alyx Hodges, for all your hours of patient, painstaking help.

Thank you also to Gary Allen, Gillian Allen, Brian Bek, Suzanne Brahm, Janet Lee Carey, Roxanne Dunn, Billee Longuski Escott, Amanda Geers, Erik Ørum Hansen, Peter Kahle, Abhijit Kini, Bharti Kirchner, Phoebe Kitanidis, Lyn Macfarlane, Kate Madrid, Divya Mallar, Kathy Manchip,

Jayant Swamy, and Lavanya Vasudevan, for your keen eyes and ideas.

I owe endless thanks to my editor, Annie Berger, my agent, Jim McCarthy, and everyone at Sourcebooks, for all your support and belief.

And to my friends, my family, my in-laws Ken and Kay who helpfully pointed out that I didn't mention them last time, and most of all, Sammy Lou, my personal firework.

About the Author

Kevin John Scott is from the oldest town in Britain. For a while, he lived in Scandinavia, the inspiration for the Frederik Sandwich stories. Today, he lives near Seattle, among yet more trees and raindrops, with his wonderful, creative, haphazard family. Visit kevinjohnscott.com or on Twitter @_kevinjohnscott.

Check out the beginning of Frederik's adventures in

FREDERIK SANDWICH and the EARTHQUAKE that Couldn't POSSIBLY BE

At the age of eleven or thereabouts, Frederik suddenly woke up. Of course, he had awoken before at a whole range of ages, three for example, eight and a half, and everything in between on an orderly, daily basis. There was nothing unusual about awakening at the age of eleven apart from the violent shaking. The bed was shaking. Violently. Like an airplane in turbulence. The whole room. Rippling and shuddering. Frederik, at first, was unruffled. He had been asleep in a world of dreams where unusual things happen all the time, and this was another unusual thing and therefore entirely to be expected. Except he was awake. When Frederik worked that out, he became rapidly ruffled after all.

The room was dark. Through slats in the blinds, streetlights made stripes on the ceiling. The stripes were vibrating.

"Aaaagh," said Frederik, to see if he could, to make sure this wasn't one of those dreams where he thought he was awake but really wasn't. But sure enough, the sound came out in a warble.

"Aaaagh," he said again, and this time it wasn't an experiment but a creeping doubt. Pictures clattered and the bed shook like a washing machine. How long had this been going on? A minute? More? He could still remember his dream and there had been no shaking—not till he awoke abruptly to find his bed on the move.

He tried to make sense of this unprecedented situation, not daring to budge. His room took up the top floor of a tall, narrow house. His parents slept four floors below in their basement bedroom—they found it cozy. Frederik meanwhile felt a glorious freedom up here in the rafters. He loved to lean from the balcony and stare over rooftops, between chimneys, tracking time by the clock tower that looked like a lighthouse but couldn't possibly be because the sea was too far away. He could gaze at the stars through his telescope and feel like he was among them, part of a never-ending, orderly pattern. Up here, there were no unpleasant neighbors, no one he had to avoid. But tonight, all alone halfway to the sky with everything rattling, he felt for the first time entirely too far from the ground.

In the shadows, he could see only shapes—the end of the bed, the wardrobe. The silhouette of his precious telescope as it fell off its stand and rolled to the edge of the dresser. He reached out a hand in dread but was too far away. The telescope tipped, a dead weight of metal and delicate glass. It hit the hardwood floor with a thud and a tinkle of broken pieces. His most treasured possession!

Frantic, frightened, and fascinated, all on top of one another, he scrambled to get up and check outside. Hesitated—afraid of what might be out there. Tanks invading the streets and shaking the city off its foundations. No. Nothing like that had happened in generations. And tanks would be noisy. Beyond the rattling blinds and his property smashing, there was no sound. No far-off rumble, no nearby clatter. No thunder, no gunfire, and still the furniture jolted as though the building had been loaded on a truck and driven down an unpaved road.

There had to be a sensible explanation, and his next thought was an earthquake. But Frederik's Hill was built on silt and sand and thousands of miles from anything so dramatic, a pimple on the lowest, dullest island of a stable, orderly nation. No faults, no rifts, no volcanoes—nothing but shallow sea and sandy soil. No earthquake had been recorded here in the history of science, and Frederik knew his science, studied it diligently. An earthquake it couldn't possibly be.

And then a terrible, new suspicion crept in under his guard.

Aliens.

Massive, silent spaceships in the sky above his bedroom, pounding the planet with wobble rays to break the spirits of the inhabitants of Earth. Tremble beams, shaking the town like a tambourine. Sinister creatures with tentacle fingers and almond-shaped eyes. The city surrounded in three dimensions, maybe more. All would perish. Skinned, pureed, and poured into a stinking vat on the mother ship to be slowly digested in the awful acid of alien stomachs. He knew this to be fanciful and foolish, but what other interpretation was there? It scared the bejeebers out of him.

He wrestled loose from the warmth of his quilt. He crawled like a commando across the bed, head low, riding the shudders that clattered his windows and toppled his belongings. He reached for the blinds, tilted the slats, and peered out through condensation and glass and cold night air.

And the trembling stopped.